Richard Carpenter's

ROBIN OF
SHERWOOD

THE HUNTRESS

Richard Carpenter's
Robin of Sherwood
The Huntress
By Jennifer Ash
Adapted from a script
by Jennifer Ash &
Barnaby Eaton-Jones
Published in 2025 by
Chinbeard Books

in association with
Oak Tree Books
oaktreebooks.uk

Editor: Barnaby Eaton-Jones
Sub Editor: Harriet Whitehouse

Richard Carpenter's

ROBIN OF SHERWOOD

THE HUNTRESS

by
Jennifer Ash

From an idea by
Barnaby Eaton-Jones

A Chinbeard Books / Oak Tree Books Original

PROLOGUE

Robin Hood and Sir Guy of Gisburne glared at each other as their swords locked. Both were all too aware of the furious clash of metal against metal coming from behind them, echoing through the forest.

A battle of strength, neither man spoke as they concentrated on not being the one to yield.

Occasionally the rapid sound of Will Scarlet's blade striking its target was punctuated by the fast, arrhythmic thud of Friar Tuck's quarterstaff against a chest or limb; an occasional grunt of exertion or cry of pain from the four men they fought, and the scuffling of feet and hooves.

His eyes never leaving his enemy, Robin heard an arrow fly from the trees, sending one of the sheriff's men falling to the unforgiving forest floor. He knew it was time to end things before another innocent soldier was hurt.

'How many times do we have to tell you, Gisburne? Sherwood is ours!'

'Yours! *Nothing* is yours, wolfshead.'

Gisburne's taunt had no sooner left his mouth, when his grip broke, and Robin had wrenched his sword from his hand.

'On your knees, Sir Guy!'

Reluctantly hitting the dusty trackway, Gisburne felt the vibration of the earth as the fight continued around them. Despite the precarious nature of his position, he couldn't resist giving Herne's Son a cruel smile. 'Your precious God is dead—and *still* you continue this pointless crusade!'

Moving with blurring speed, Robin pressed the tip of his sword, Albion, against his opponent's chest. 'I never thought you'd resort to childish lies, Gisburne. Have some pride, man.'

With triumphant relish, Guy taunted, 'Don't tell me Herne's Son doesn't know the fate of his master?'

As a well-aimed arrow from the trees sent another soldier needing his arm in a sling for the next several weeks, Robin growled, 'I'm warning you, Gisburne...'

'I've *seen* him, Loxley! His body lies dead; washed up in that pathetic cave of his.'

Spinning around fast, Robin grabbed Gisburne by the throat, lifting him up so they were face to face. He shouted at the top of his voice, 'EVERYONE STOP!'

The fight faltered to a standstill. It only took a split second for the two remaining, uninjured soldiers to see that, once again, their leader had been overcome by the Hooded Man.

As they lowered their swords, Marion came out of the trees, her bow still drawn. Tuck kept his quarterstaff held out before him, while Will weighed his blade in his hand, watching everywhere at once, just in case the ceasefire should fail.

'Pick yourself up and get out of here. Take your men with you before I allow Scarlet to kill the lot of you.'

'Chance would be a fine thing.' Will glowered in hatred at the man slowly rising from the forest floor.

'Go on! Leave.' Robin yelled at Gisburne. 'Now!'

The outlaws remained silent as they watched the sheriff's men hastily mount their horses and gallop away. As soon as they were out of sight, Robin turned his back on the roadside clearing and strode purposely into the forest, his face creased with concern.

It was Marion who asked the question on everyone's mind. 'Robin, what is it? What's wrong?'

'Herne—he's called me. I must go.'

'I didn't hear him.'

'He spoke to me alone.' Robin reached out a hand to Marion. 'I have to go. You head back with the others; I'll see you there.'

Convinced Robin wasn't telling her all he knew, Marion persisted. 'I think one of us should go with you.'

'I'm going alone.' Without a backward glance at his wife, Robin disappeared into the depths of Sherwood.

Stabbing the air with his knife, Will snapped, 'Well, that's us told.'

'He'll have his reasons for going alone.'

'For Heaven's sake, Marion!' Will gave her a pitiful look. 'He *always* has his reasons. Never mind the rest of us.'

Puffing hard as he got his breath back, Tuck rested against his staff. 'We ought to do what Robin says, Scarlet.'

'We *always* do what Robin says. Why doesn't he just ask our opinion!?'

Tuck shrugged. 'If Herne has called Robin, there's nothing we can do until they've spoken.

Anyway, it's high time I put the stew on, or they'll be no supper later.'

Will continued to grumble as he followed Tuck through the trees. They'd only gone a few yards when Marion stopped abruptly, patting at the folds of her cloak.

'I'll have to catch up with you. I've left my knife behind. Must have dropped it in the fight.'

'You want me to help you look, Little Flower?'

'No, I'll be fine. I won't be long. You carry on with supper. At least we'll have more to eat this week.'

Tuck grinned as he thought of their temporarily absent companions. 'I packed some cold meat for John and Much. They won't go hungry either. Nasir said he would feed off the forest.'

Scarlet stared through the trees, as if trying to work out where Robin had gone. 'I should have gone with 'em, instead of Nasir.'

Marion flicked her long russet ponytail over her shoulder. 'If you had, we'd have been in trouble back there. You fought like you had the Devil in you, Will.'

'I had to make up for the three of them deserting us, didn't I? Picked a fine time to wander off on a pilgrimage.'

Tuck tutted. 'Hardly a pilgrimage, Will. They're not going on a religious quest.'

Increasing his pace, Will Scarlet trudged faster. 'That ain't entirely true, is it? John's uncle's a priest.'

'Well, yes.' Tuck admitted.

'And he's missing.'

'Again… yes.'

Scarlet prodded Tuck in the back, 'Well, finding a priest is a pilgrimage in my book.'

Marion grinned, 'He's got a point, Tuck.'

'I thought you were going to retrieve your knife, Little Flower.'

'I'm going, I'm going.'

As Marion ran back the way they'd come, Friar Tuck slapped Will on the shoulder. 'Now, come along, you heathen. Let me explain to you what a pilgrimage is…'

'Oh, Lord help us.'

'He usually does, Will. He usually does…'

The tread of Robin's feet against the uneven floor echoed around the cave.

'Herne? Are you here?'

Pausing to listen for any sign of movement, all Robin could hear was the trickle of water coursing down the walls, before it dripped into puddle-like pools upon the floor.

He moved deeper into the cave, feeling the air change around him. It chilled Robin from the inside out; every sense telling him that something was wrong.

'Herne! No!' Robin called out in alarm as he rushed towards the fallen body beside the cave's altar. 'I'll kill Gisburne for this… Herne? Can you get up?' Kneeling, he reached out his hands. 'It's wet on the floor. Let me help you up and…'

Robin abruptly let go of the body, startled by what he saw. 'Oh!'

Instinct made him draw Albion, holding its comforting weight in his hands, as he backed away. 'Who are you? Where's Herne?'

Slowly, the figure in front of Robin unfolded. The voice, when it eventually spoke, seemed to come from far away—yet its echo still filled the cave; steady and sure.

'Put that sword away and kneel Herne's Son—I am the Huntress, and you shall do my bidding…'

CHAPTER ONE

The sound of the Sheriff of Nottingham slamming his goblet against the high table was almost lost amongst the noisy bustle of Nottingham Castle's great hall.

'For God's sake, Hugo! It's hardly my fault Fairfax survived.'

'I never said it was your fault, brother!' Abbot Hugo spoke through gritted teeth. 'Pour me some wine, Gisburne!'

'Yes, my Lord.'

The sheriff clenched his jaw. 'And you could try not sounding so miserable, Gisburne!'

'I'm no more miserable than you, my Lord.'

The sheriff thumped a fist against the arm of his chair. 'We are all disappointed that Peter Fairfax didn't obligingly get killed on the battlefields of France, but as he's due here to dine with us any minute now, we need to at least pretend to be pleased to see him.'

Abbot Hugo grumbled into his goblet. 'I suppose so.'

'We don't want him changing his will, do we. After all, he won't live forever, and then his lands *will* be ours.'

Gisburne took a sip of wine. 'I'll drink to that.'

Robert de Rainault scowled. 'No, you won't. You'll go and wait by the door to welcome our honoured guest, and escort him in.'

This time it was his deputy's turn to bang his goblet onto the table. 'Yes, my Lord.'

As his deputy stalked off, the sheriff gave a wry smile. 'Temper, temper, Gisburne.'

The droplets of the water falling, with an almost musical regularity from the cave's roof, accompanied the tempo of Robin's heartbeat as he gaped at the figure before him.

'Approach me, Herne's Son.'

Swallowing against the lump that had formed in his throat, Robin peered around him, unable to stop hoping that he'd see Herne appear. As the seconds ticked past, and the Lord of the Trees remained silent, Robin finally accepted that his guide wasn't coming to help him and addressed the woman with open caution.

'You are the Huntress? Herne did not tell me about you.'

'He trusts that you do not need to know everything of his realm.'

Taken aback, Robin whispered, '*You* are from the realm of the forest?'

'I am from Herne.'

Crouching down, the Huntress focused on one of the many puddles that dotted the cave's uneven floor. Then, taking a vial from the folds of her deerskin cloak, she poured its contents into the water.

'I bid you approach, Hooded Man.'

'Are you going to show me Herne in a *puddle*? Where is he?'

Unruffled, the Huntress focused on what she was doing. 'I am going to show you what you need to see. Look now—stare into the water that pools the cave floor.' The puddle began to bubble and spit. 'Watch, Herne's Son… eyes alert. Explain to me what the water shows you.'

Kneeling closer, Robin heard the rickety whirr of wooden wheels fill the cave. A second later, the pool stilled, showing the source of the sound. 'There's a cart. It's travelling across Sherwood… it's on the road from Wickham to Nottingham…' Robin drew in a sharp breath as the water issued an angry hissing noise, as if it was commentating on the picture it was revealing. 'A man has run from the woods. An outlaw?'

Robin raked a hand through his hair as he saw the cart's driver tug sharply on his reins, bringing the horse to a halt as the stranger, his face set in determination, sprinted forward.

'He's… he's attacking the cart… there are two people…'

Screams and shouts of terror made the pool's water shake.

'The driver—a man—he's fallen. I think he's dead. I…'

The water crackled and spat as the scene changed.

Was that an arrow? Robin lifted his eyes from the vision. 'Wait… I haven't seen it all yet… the picture's changing…'

The Huntress said nothing as the background

noise blended slowly from the attack to the movement of horses and men at arms.

Forcing his attention back to the pool, Robin cleared his throat. 'Nottingham Castle... Gisburne... He's in the stables... Who's he talking to? I can't see... it's a nobleman. No... it's the man who attacked the cart...'

Robin stepped back, his head suddenly thumping with a dull ache. 'Why are you showing me this? Where's Herne? Why...?'

The background rippling of the pool calmed as the cave vibrated with a reassuring voice. A voice Robin was very glad to hear.

'Do her bidding, my son... trust her... you must trust her...'

'Herne!' Robin moved further from the puddle, whirling around in the hope of seeing the Lord of the Trees.

'Look back into the water, my son...'

Obeying immediately, Robin saw the pool water crackle and clear, taking him back into the vision.

'It's the cart that was attacked... there are two bodies.' Helpless rage rang in his voice as he saw the lifeless figures. 'He's killed them both!'

With a clap of The Huntress's hands, the puddle calmed. 'It has been shown.'

Moving away from the pool with more confidence than before, Robin asked, 'What am I meant to do?'

'Bring them justice. In mercy there is justice…'

'And Herne?'

The Huntress raised her arms out to her sides as she declared, 'My bidding is his bidding.'

Robin was oblivious to the singing of the birds in the trees as he made his way back to the camp. He walked slowly, trapped in thought. It was only instinct that sent his hand to Albion as a woman stepped out of the trees before him.

'Robin?'

'I told you to go back to the camp, Marion.' Robin wasn't sure if he was relieved or annoyed that she'd ignored his request to stay with the others.

'I know. You've got to be careful about always ordering everyone around. It's sometimes a little harsh.' Not comfortable with the doubts that troubled her, she asked, 'Have you really been with Herne? There was something not right about how you left earlier.'

'I've just been to his cave.'

Marion recognised the evasive lilt to his tone. 'What is it you're not telling us this time?'

'I always tell you…'

'No, you don't!' Marion cut in angrily. 'Don't you see! You *need* us, Robin. It's dangerous to act alone. But if you aren't always honest about what you're doing, how can we help you when things go wrong?'

'It isn't always safe to tell you.'

'We aren't children! Think Robin! Don't give Will cause to doubt that we work best as a group. We're either in this together, or we're not.'

Knowing his wife was right, Robin slipped a hand into hers. 'I'm sorry. Do the others know you are here?'

'I told them I'd lost my knife and was going back to find it.'

'I see…' Robin gently cupped her chin with his free hand as he gave her a wry smile. 'So, *you* didn't tell them what you were doing then?'

'Well, I…'

Robin laughed. 'Let's get back. I'll talk to everyone.'

After only a few steps, Robin stumbled to a halt. A rush of cold consumed him as the vision he'd just seen flashed back through his mind. Giving Marion's hand a parting squeeze, he let go. 'We should hurry...' He broke into a run. '...I've a feeling that time is against us. Or, at least, it's against Herne.'

Not giving his fellow outlaws time to comment on his sudden disappearance after their encounter with Gisburne and his men, Robin called them together as he and Marion arrived in the camp's clearing.

As Tuck handed around some food and drink, the four friends huddled by the fire. Will, Tuck and Marion waited, with varying levels of patience, as they watched Robin of Loxley mutely study the dancing flames.

His mind full of all he'd seen and heard while he was with the Huntress, it was a while before Robin finally spoke. 'In the cave—it wasn't Herne.'

Tuck selected a piece of pork from his wooden trencher. 'What do you mean?'

'Gisburne told me that Herne was dead. That's why I went. I needed to...'

Will interrupted, his quick to ignite temper, instantly at boiling point. 'You should have told us!

Taken us with you. Anyone could have been waiting for you? It could have been one of Gisburne's traps!'

Robin took hold of Marion's hand as Will Scarlet reacted just as she'd predicted he would. 'Scarlet, I did what I thought was best. What if...?'

But Will was not in the mood to listen. 'What is this? There's always an excuse with you! I thought we'd sorted this! If you have a problem with us helping you, Robin, then...'

Marion's arm darted forwards. She grabbed the nearest log and threw it onto the fire, the resulting crackle and shooting of the flames cutting through Scarlet's increasing ire. 'Then it's a problem we need to deal with later, Will. There's a bigger problem for us to worry about for the moment. Tell them, Robin.'

Robin cleared his throat. 'Herne might not have been in the cave, but someone else was...'

CHAPTER TWO

Despite the troubling reason for his return to Derbyshire, Little John couldn't help but smile as the outline of Hathersage appeared in the distance. As he and his friends, Much and Nasir, reached a row of fields where the local lord's sheep roamed, he realised he was looking forward to showing them where he'd grown up.

'It only seems a moment since I worked here as a lad.'

'I can't imagine you as a shepherd.' Much smiled. 'Very different from being an outlaw.'

'In some ways, but I was still protecting things— just sheep, not people. Wolves aren't that different from most criminals, really—they both steal because they are hungry. It's about survival. In fact, wolves are far better than a lot of people. Wolves *never* kill because they're greedy, or cruel, or for fun.'

With a short grunt of agreement, Nasir scanned the path ahead. 'You know where to go?'

Scrubbing a hand through his unruly mop of hair, John had to admit that he didn't. 'I suppose the most obvious place to start searching for my uncle would be the inn.'

Much was surprised. 'The inn, not the church?'

'I'm sure the locals will have checked the church for him many times. Anyway, the inn was always Uncle Harold's favourite place.'

Nasir gave a wry smile as Much said, 'Priests aren't supposed to drink—are they?'

Little John chuckled. 'You clearly don't know many priests, lad.'

'But the church says…'

'It says, as far as I know, that they can drink, but they aren't *supposed* to get drunk, lad.' John winked, 'but don't tell Tuck.'

'I wish the others were with us.' Much stared across the open fields to either side of them. The lack of forest cover was making him feel vulnerable.

Still hurt that Robin had said they couldn't all leave Sherwood to help search for his missing uncle, John chose not to mull over the argument that had followed the departure of the messenger who'd come from Hathersage to find him.

John wished he hadn't got angry—hadn't thrown the fact that, not so long ago, they'd gone out of their way to help Marion's father in Robin's face. He gave an internal wince as he remembered how he'd shouted, '*You willingly crossed England as far as the coast for your wife's sake… but you won't even travel to the next county to help me.*'

He felt his cheeks redden and his heart become heavy as he forced himself to accept that Herne's Son, even after all they'd been through together, wouldn't leave Sherwood for him.

John's reply was designed to convince himself as well as Much. 'It wouldn't have been right to leave the forest unprotected, even though we work better together.'

'Robin said he'd be needed.' Nasir was resolute.

'He couldn't say why, though.' John sighed.

'He was sure.'

'Ay, Nas, he was.' John drew a ragged breath, 'and annoyingly, he's usually right.'

Flicking his astute gaze from one companion to the other, Nasir drew their attention to a fork in the pathway ahead.

'Left will take us into the heart of Hathersage,' John waved his quarterstaff out before them. 'While the other road would take us to the church and on to the local sheriff's manor house and the road to Chesterfield.'

'Then we go left.' Nasir started towards the trackway.

As they walked, John mulled over what Thomas, the messenger who'd come all the way to Sherwood from Hathersage, had told him.

Your uncle's not been seen for days, John... Sunday came and went and there was no service in the church. The tavern is not the same without his off-key singing... We've had men out looking for 'im—but there's no sign and the sheriff... he don't want to know.... Not with Harold being related to you like...

Thomas had coloured bright red, but not as red as Will Scarlet, who'd had something choice to say about officials who made assumptions about people because of who they were related to.

John bit back his own anger as he reflected further on Thomas's message.

...The thing is John... there's these two men... beyond saving the pair of 'em. Been robbing from the town, though they's got no need too. Do it for fun, the locals reckon, but your uncle... he was sure he could make 'em see sense... went looking for 'em... but that was days back and we ain't seen him since...

Dismissing the sense of foreboding that trickled

up his spine, John strode forwards. 'We'll probably find Thomas in his workshop. Let's see if he can tell us anything else useful.'

The scent of wet clay filled the air as the three outlaws entered the potter's workshop.

As the newcomers cast a light over the poorly lit space, Thomas looked up, a grin crossing his round face. 'John! I'm so glad you're here! Thank you!'

'I'm sorry I couldn't come at once, but there were things I needed to do back home first.' John could feel Much's eyes on his back, and knew that, he too, was also remembering the argument that had delayed their departure.

'Sherwood relies on you all, we understand that.' Thomas's expression became more serious as he smeared his clay-stained hands down his apron. 'I'm glad you came, though… just the three of you? Yes?'

'Yes.' John gestured to his friends. 'Still no sign of Uncle Harold?'

Thomas kept his eyes fixed on the pot he was moulding into shape. 'Not a trace. It's like he's vanished into thin air.'

Much shuddered. 'You don't think he has, do you?'

John placed a reassuring hand on Much's shoulder, 'People don't just vanish.'

'They might do if a sorcerer or...'

'This won't be sorcery. I'm sure it won't.' Hoping he was right about that, John turned back to the potter. 'So, any news since we spoke in Sherwood?'

'I was asking in the tavern.' Thomas smoothed a hand over the clay vessel. 'The two men I told you about, they were causing trouble in the market the other day. Knocking over stalls and the like. Your uncle was determined to talk to them, make 'em see sense. He followed them into the fields towards Dawnhill Wood.'

'And then what happened?' Much asked.

'No one knows.' Thomas blushed, 'I'm ashamed to say that no one went with him.'

John stared towards the door, seeing the fields beyond in his mind's eye. 'Uncle Harold would never have let anyone go with him anyway. Stubborn as a mule... and brave too...'

'Like you.' Nasir gave John a teasing smile.

'Stubborn? Me?'

Much chuckled, 'You maybe are a bit... not like Will is, though.'

'I should think not, lad.' John looked up at the potter. 'What can you tell us about these two troublemakers, Thomas?'

CHAPTER THREE

The Sheriff of Nottingham leant back so that a servant could recharge his goblet with claret. Glancing at his brother out of the corner of his eye, communicating his unspoken, but obvious, opinion about their rather ill-at-ease guest, he raised his drink in a toast.

'We are most relieved to have you here with us, my Lord Fairfax. So many do not return from the French wars.'

Peter Fairfax inclined his head. 'Your concern is an honour, my Lord Sheriff. The battlefield is a merciless place.'

Giving his deputy a thin smile, the sheriff's voice was silky smooth. 'Gisburne, here, feared for you. He was worried about the future of your lands should the worst have happened.'

'Huh!' Gisburne snorted into his wine.

Annoyed at his companion's lack of subtly, the sheriff snapped, 'Pour us more wine, Gisburne.'

As his cup was refilled, Lord Fairfax surveyed the hall at large. 'Thank you, Sir Guy. You're wise to have settled for a life here, instead of fighting in France.'

Abbot Hugo's sullen contemplation was punctuated by a cruel laugh. 'Gisburne wouldn't last five minutes outside of Nottingham.'

'My Lord Abbot, I must protest! I...'

The sheriff waved a dismissive hand. 'Yes, yes, Gisburne... I'm sure you'd be a *marvel* on the battlefields. So, Lord Fairfax...'

'Please, my Lord, call me Peter.'

'Peter then, what are your plans now you are returned to us?'

Leaning across the table, Peter's hand quivered as he confided, 'You know, of course, that my parents were murdered.'

Hugo's eyebrows rose as he exchanged a more obvious glance with his brother. 'Murdered?'

The sheriff frowned. 'I'd heard something about them having had an accident on their way to visit me...' He paused to take a drink. 'Remember, Hugo? They were coming to discuss our agreement concerning the inheritance of their lands, should Peter here die in battle.'

Hugo muttered, 'I can't say I do, but...'

The abbot got no further, as the sheriff switched his attention back to Peter. 'I assumed the accident was hearsay and that they simply hadn't bothered to turn up.'

Moving with startling speed, a furious Peter scraped his chair back so that its legs screeched against the stone floor. He leapt to his feet, his words infused with passion. 'No, my Lords! They were killed—murdered! By Robin Hood.'

In an instant, Gisburne's waning interest in the discussion was triggered into angry urgency. 'If that wolfshead has done this, then he *must* pay, my Lord!'

Rolling his eyes, Robert de Rainault waved to the nearest servant to come and refill his wine. 'Yes, yes, Gisburne, of course he must. We'll track them down.'

'Not *them*, my Lord—just him. It was Robin Hood.' Peter urged.

'On his own? Are you sure?' Hugo felt the need to shuffle his chair a few inches back from Fairfax. Something about the young man was strangely unsettling.

Slapping his hand upon the table, Peter growled, 'You question my word, my Lord Abbot?'

'Of course not.'

Privately enjoying how uncomfortable his brother appeared, the sheriff patted a hand on the back of the nearest chair, and coaxed, 'Do sit down, Peter.'

Doing as he was bidden, the young Lord Fairfax gave his host an apologetic smile.

Hiding his relief, the sheriff adopted a conciliatory manner. 'Now, Peter, you must understand that capturing Robin Hood is not as straightforward as it...'

'I *shall* capture him!' Completely missing the sheriff's attempts to calm their guest and his warning glare, Gisburne ploughed on. 'I can assure you, Lord Fairfax, that your parents' death will be avenged.'

'Thank you, Sir Guy, but there is no need to risk the lives of your men. What's done is done. No amount of revenge will bring back the dead—I learnt that the hard way in France.' Peter put down his goblet with care, all signs of his previous frustration gone, as if a switch had flipped in his mind. 'I only told you, so you'd know of his latest outrage. Plus, well—I wouldn't want their deaths to be dismissed as an accident.'

'Indeed, Peter...' Lifting a slice of meat from the platter before them, the sheriff smiled, '...a refreshing attitude, and one which, as you say, spares my men the risk of having an arrow in their backs.'

With a brief dip of his head, Lord Peter Fairfax got back to his feet. 'Now, if you'll excuse me, my Lords, I must return to my manor. With my parents gone, there is much to do.'

The De Rainault brothers and Gisburne stood as their guest prepared to take his leave. The sheriff raised an arm towards Hugo. 'Perhaps you would permit the abbot and Gisburne to escort you through the forest. Hugo is heading back to St Mary's now, *aren't* you, brother?'

'If you say so, Robert.'

'Your consideration is welcomed.' Peter gave a bow of appreciation in the direction of the De Rainaults. 'Thank you, my Lords.'

'I intended to visit the chapel before we go. I will meet you both in the stables; Lord Fairfax, Gisburne.' Abbot Hugo gave the sheriff a penetrating glare as he drifted towards the heart of the castle. 'Until next time, brother.'

Watching the abbot depart, Robert de Rainault mumbled, 'I always worry when Hugo feels the need to pray, makes me wonder what he's up to.'

'My Lord?' Peter took a step nearer to the sheriff.

'Oh. Nothing. Just a bit of sibling rivalry.'

'I never had a brother.'

De Rainault snorted. 'Count yourself lucky.'

Peter looked as if he counted himself less than lucky. 'Or a sister.'

'Doubly lucky.'

'I used to fight with a girl who came to court. She was a firecracker. Needed to be taught a lesson.'

The sheriff picked his goblet back up. 'I find that women, Peter, prefer to do the teaching. That is why I will never marry. I don't need a power behind the throne. I'm quite powerful enough without having someone nag me from behind. I get enough of that from Gisburne. Don't I, Sir Guy?'

'If you say so, my Lord,' Gisburne sneered as he thumped back onto his seat.

Peter's voice suddenly wavered with emotion and through gritted teeth, he hissed. 'It will be good to reclaim *my* throne. To have power again. To rule over what is rightfully mine.'

'And we hope you do so for as long as you live, Peter. Amen.' Not wanting Lord Fairfax to either wallow in his misery or flip back into anger, the sheriff brought them back to the point. 'Now, if you head to the stables, Gisburne will meet you there in a moment. I need to have a quick word with him first.'

'Thank you for your hospitality, my Lord.'

Waiting until Peter was out of earshot, the sheriff came to Gisburne's side. He spoke quietly.

'How fortunate it was that young Fairfax survived his experiences in France.'

Understanding his master's meaning at once, Gisburne kept his reply deadpan. 'Most fortunate, my Lord.'

'Then, wouldn't it be a shame if a fatal misfortune met him now that he's back.'

'Tragic, my Lord.' Gisburne was already lowering his goblet and reaching for his cloak.

'See to it, Gisburne.'

'Yes, my Lord.'

The sheriff gave a thin smile. 'I've already ordered enough claret to fill the Fairfax cellars. If this all goes to plan, I might even let you have some of it.'

Fastening his cloak, Gisburne grunted, 'Good of you, my Lord.'

The musty scent of straw and horses hit Gisburne as he entered the stables of Nottingham Castle. He took a moment to savour the scene. Men-at-arms and stable hands were moving between the horses, grooming, tacking up and readying themselves for the afternoon ahead. This was where he felt at his most in control. Horses never argued with you, they never sniped back with sarcastic comments.

His moment of peace diminished when he saw Lord Peter Fairfax mounting his horse at the far side of the stable block, with the familiar figure of Abbot Hugo bustled into the stall next to him, before being hoisted onto his horse by two hefty stable hands.

Swiftly mounting his own steed, Gisburne followed a handful of soldiers, Abbot Hugo and Peter from the stables. As they reached the castle's courtyard, Sir Guy rode up to Peter's side. 'You may not wish to avenge that cursed wolfshead, my Lord Fairfax, but he's been avenged, nonetheless. Robin Hood will not be so full of himself from now on.'

Abbot Hugo's eyes narrowed. 'Whatever are you talking about, Gisburne?'

Not even attempting to keep the smugness from his voice, Gisburne relished his words. 'Herne the Hunter is dead.'

The abbot reined in his horse so fast that the whole party came to an abrupt halt in a confusion of whinnies and stamped hooves.

'What have you done, Gisburne? Haven't I warned you about playing with things you don't understand?'

Cool in the face of Abbot Hugo's unease, Gisburne smirked. 'I've done nothing but make a fortunate discovery, my Lord. Their forest God is no more.'

Peter looked searchingly at his companions. 'I know little of this forest God you speak of. Maybe you can tell me all you know of Robin Hood and his 'god', once we're out of the castle.'

'Certainly, my Lord.' Gisburne threw the abbot a superior glare as he pressed his horse forward.

Abbot Hugo bit his lips together. The familiar rhythm of their horses' hooves clattering across the stone floor did nothing to calm the disquiet that filled him as he followed Gisburne and the volatile Lord Peter Fairfax towards the castle's gateway.

CHAPTER FOUR

'I don't like the sound of the men Thomas was talking about, Little John.'

'Nor do I, Much.' John passed a flagon of ale to Nasir as they sat in the far corner of the local tavern. 'But one thing's for certain, my uncle was right about them needing to be taught a lesson.'

'It won't be easy.' Nasir refused the ale, taking an apple from his pocket instead. 'Noblemen believe they can do anything.'

'Do you think they'll come tonight?' Much glanced nervously towards the door.

'Thomas said they like to make a nuisance of themselves in here sometimes… but not every evening.'

'It's early yet. We need to be patient.' Crunching into his apple, Nasir watched the tavern's customers as they came and went, taking no heed of the number of curious glances and passing comments the presence of a Saracen in their inn was causing.

Knowing Nasir was right, John resigned himself to waiting to see if anything happened, or if they could overhear anything that might be helpful to them. After an hour had passed, however, John muttered under his breath, 'We won't be able to stay here too much longer. It's only a matter of time until word that three outlaws are in Hathersage reaches the local sheriff—De Grange, his name is. Father of the men who might have hurt my uncle.'

Much gulped. 'We should find somewhere to hide.'

'We will.' John felt his gaze drawn to the flames of the fire on the opposite side of the inn; they reminded him of home. Of the camp. Of where he knew what to do when things went wrong. 'If these men haven't arrived by the time we've finished our drinks, then we'll think of a new plan.'

As the three friends lapsed into silence, John considered everything Thomas had told them.

The men who'd be causing so much disruption were De Grange's two youngest sons. John vaguely remembered them from his youth, but they'd been just children when he'd last lived in Hathersage, and firmly under their father's control. If Thomas was to be believed, they'd grown into disruptive youths, with a sense of entitlement that was all too familiar with the nobility in recent years. They had made a game out of stealing from the local workshops, damaging goods on market stands, and taunting the local population; not caring who they hurt, and with no fear of any consequences.

As if reading John's thoughts, Much asked, 'Why would they want to damage the stalls in the market? If the people can't sell their produce, then the lord won't get his share. Wouldn't that make their father poorer—as well as the market holders they're attacking, I mean?'

'It would. But people with money don't see things like that. What's a few pennies robbed from a butcher to them, when they are secure in their lands?'

Much could just imagine what their friends in Sherwood would think about such behaviour. 'Robin would say they needed teaching a lesson.'

'And he'd be right, lad... but how? That's the question. And have they really got something to do with my uncle's disappearance, or is this just a coincidence?' John's stomach clenched into knots as he contemplated what might have happened to his kin. Lords Aidan and Henry are sons from their father's second marriage. They have two older brothers who will inherit the lordship and most of the lands.'

'They act through frustration.' Nasir murmured. 'They search for a place in life.'

'Probably. But they shouldn't be doing it like this.'

As Nasir gave a tiny nod of agreement, Much ventured, 'Father Harold sounds very brave. I'm sure he'll be alright.'

'Thanks, Much, but I'll still be happier when he's safely back in Hathersage.'

'Where do we start looking for him, though?'

'Let's cross the fields, to Dawnhill. That's where my uncle said he was planning to follow the troublemakers.' John swigged some of his ale. 'I'm not sure we should have come here first, after all. Perhaps we should have headed to the church, just to double check he hasn't gone back there, and then headed towards Dawnhill as soon as Thomas told us where he'd last been seen...'

'We were tired and hungry.' Much tried to reassure Little John. 'Better that we rested first.'

Nasir agreed, but John was restless. 'These are the decisions Robin must make all the time. I don't envy him.'

Much gave a small chuckle. 'Try telling Will that!'

John grinned. 'He doesn't find taking orders easy. How he managed as a soldier, I can't imagine.'

'He don't talk about his time in France a lot, does he.'

'War changes people, Much. It can make them into people they don't like... Scarlet battles with that, although he'd never admit it. He...' John stopped talking as the door to the tavern opened, bringing in both a cutting draught and two well-dressed young men.

'Is that them?' Much mouthed quietly as they saw the locals becoming intent on their drinks while the volume of the previously animated conversation plummeted.

Much's question was answered for him when the taller of the two men slammed a hand down against the bar and bellowed into the innkeeper's face.

'Claret, man. Now!'

Holding his ground, the innkeeper squared his shoulders. 'My Lord Aidan, Lord Henry, I've explained to you before, we serve ale here. If you wish to drink claret, then you should return to the manor.'

'Do you hear that, brother?' Henry sneered, 'We are to go home to quench our thirst.'

'How rude.' Aidan fixed his thin grey eyes on the innkeeper. 'Any sensible barman would make sure that he has the drinks his customer requested ready in his cellar. Especially customers whose father happens to be the local sheriff.'

'Rude and foolish, brother.'

The hush that had blanketed the tavern when the noblemen had entered had now frozen into an icy, fearful, silence. There was no sound but for the crackle of the fire and the gentle whistle of the breeze outside, as it crept through the knotholes in the door and the gaps in the shuttered windows.

'We warned you on our last visit that we would not be pleased to have our requests denied again.' Aidan produced a short dagger from his belt, giving a bark of laughter as he saw the innkeeper's face go pale. 'I do believe our host is afraid of us, Henry.'

'And yet, if he'd been a good boy and done as he was told, then resorting to threats with my dagger wouldn't have been necessary.' Aidan toyed the knife from palm to palm. 'So, landlord, what are we to do about this situation?'

Henry's second bark of humourless laughter was cut short as he became acutely aware of the blade of a sword being tapped against his shoulder. Spinning around, his eyes travelled upwards to Little John's less than amused countenance.

Seeing his brother's alarmed expression, Aidan spun round, and found himself face to face with a calmly smiling Nasir, a shiny knife in his hand. 'What is the meaning of this?'

'I was about to ask you the same question?' John lowered his sword but kept it in his hand.

'We're in a tavern! What do you think we were doing?' Henry growled.

'It's as we always thought, brother, the peasants here have no intellect whatsoever.' Aidan glared at Nasir. 'And the calibre of person allowed to drink in this inn has reached an all-time low.'

John heard Much gasp from where he sat. Nasir, however, remained perfectly still, his knife blade doing all his talking for him, as it reflected the glow of the firelight.

Little John found himself privately giving the brothers credit, however begrudgingly, for having the courage not to back away.

They're either brave, or they are as stupid as they are arrogant.

'Landlord,' John smiled at their host, 'please pour these gentlemen some ale. I think they might need a drink.'

'We asked for…'

'Claret. Yes we heard you, lad. And yet we, like you, know that such a drink is not served here, so you will buy a tankard of ale each and be grateful.'

'Grateful!' Lord Aidan spat the word as if the concept was foreign to him.

John glanced at Much, who was still sitting at the table they'd occupied before. 'And then, once you have paid for your ale, and said thank you to the innkeeper, you will go and join our friend over there.'

'How dare…!'

Henry's sentence was cut drastically short by the rapid rise of John's sword to his throat.

'I said, pay for the ale, say thank you, and go and sit down. Yes?'

Henry's eyes narrowed, as he reluctantly said, 'Yes.'

Aidan, his cheeks burning red with anger, pulled two pennies from his cloak and banged them onto the bar, trying not to see the glee in the landlord's eyes as he wordlessly poured two tankards of ale, and passed them to his latest customers.

'That's better.' John smiled, 'Now then, let's go and sit down. We want a word with you two.'

CHAPTER FIVE

'Are you sure Gisburne's going to come out of the castle, Robin?' Friar Tuck crouched between Marion and Will Scarlet as they watched Nottingham Castle from the edge of Sherwood Forest.

'He has to eventually, and I've…' Robin caught the expression on Scarlet's face and hastily added, '…*we've*—got questions for him.'

Marion gave him an encouraging smile. 'Questions like, how Gisburne came to be in Herne's cave in the first place?'

'Yeah.' Will scratched thoughtfully at his stubble-coated chin. 'How did he even find it, Robin?'

'That's what I want to ask him.'

Tuck waved a hand towards the castle. 'We'll soon find out. Look. Here they come.'

As one, the outlaws observed Gisburne, Abbot Hugo and another man, clearly a noble, leaving the castle with a guard of a dozen soldiers behind them.

'Gisburne *and* the Abbot Hugo.' Tuck mused.

Scarlet muttered, 'Must be our lucky day.'

Creeping forwards, taking care not to make a sound, Robin studied the mounted party carefully. 'The man with them—that's him! From the vision.'

Marion joined Robin. 'The one the Huntress showed you?'

'Yes. The one who attacked the cart. We should follow him.' Standing upright, Robin hooked his bow over his shoulder. 'Well, I think we ought to—what do you all think?'

'What?' Will tutted impatiently. 'Of course we should follow him. What you asking us that for?'

Answering before Robin could voice an exasperated response, Marion said, 'Because, Will, you don't like it when Robin decides stuff without asking us.'

'Nor do you.'

'So, Robin's asking us all.'

Scarlet's gaze moved from Marion to Robin and back again. 'Yeah… right… okay.'

Robin stared along the road. He spoke fast. 'Well, do we follow? Because they're getting ahead of us.'

Tutting even louder than Will had done, Marion strode off. 'We follow. Let's go!' She'd only taken a few paces when she understood the reason for Robin's urgency before. 'Oh, typical. There's a crossroads.' She raised her arms in frustration. 'Which way?'

'This is when Nasir would have come in handy. Never mind, I'll channel him and check.'

Ignoring the collective disbelief that went with him suggesting such a thing, Tuck scouted forwards, with Robin not far behind him.

Will grumbled under his breath. 'We're wasting time, Marion. Who has discussions at a time like this?!'

'You can't have it both ways, Will. You either want Robin to ask us our opinion, or you don't.'

'But…' Will broke off as they all heard the approaching sound of Tuck as he panted and puffed his way back to them at a steady trot.

Gesturing for them to follow, he wheezed, 'This way. Come on.'

Will's eyebrows rose. 'Nasir's taught you well. All you need now is to grow what he laughingly refers to as a beard, lose some weight, and talk less.'

Tuck chuckled happily, 'Well, that's not likely to happen, is it?'

Moving in silence and taking advantage of their extensive knowledge of the forest's many shortcuts and trackways, the outlaws swiftly made up the ground between themselves and the party of soldiers ahead.

Marion pushed her long plait between the folds of her cloak as she observed the activity ahead of them. 'Looks like they're heading out of Sherwood.'

Tuck nodded. 'Towards Southwell.'

'That's where the Fairfax family have lands...' Marion paused, 'I wonder... could that be Peter?'

Robin kept his scrutinized the man he'd seen in the vision the Huntress had shown him. 'You know him?'

'I've not seen Peter since I was a child... but it could be him. He was not a nice boy—yanked at my hair and kicked my shins when he didn't get his own way. Which was a lot.'

'Charming.' Scarlet couldn't help but grin as he added, 'Did it work, though?'

'As if, Will. I kneed him right in the...'

Tuck moved forward fast, standing between

Scarlet and Marion. 'Gisburne's taken them off the main road.'

'What's he up to?'

'Should we follow him, Robin?'

'No, I don't think…. um… What do *you* all think?'

Will threw his hands upwards. 'Oh, for heaven's sake!'

Tuck rounded on his friend. 'Heaven has nothing to do with it, Scarlet. We want to talk to Gisburne, don't we? So best we wait—he'll have to come back this way to go to Nottingham.'

Marion agreed. 'And if that *is* Peter Fairfax, then he'll be heading to his manor. If we want to visit him, we can do it once we know Gisburne and the abbot are not with him.'

'That's exactly what I was going to say.' Robin smiled. 'Let's get further undercover for now. Marion, you can take first turn as lookout—if that's okay with you?'

'Of course it is. Now, I just need a leg up into this tree…'

Once Marion was safely sat in the bows of the canopy above them, Robin wandered further along the road to watch from a different angle, while Tuck and Will sat down.

Muttering quietly, Will asked, 'Are we going to have a discussion every bloomin' time we do something now, Tuck?'

The friar chuckled. 'Hasn't anyone ever told you to be careful what you wish for, Will?'

As the trackway that would take them to Fairfax House narrowed, the group of travellers adopted a single file formation, each horse walking nose-to-tail with the one in front of the other.

Abbot Hugo peered warily into the trees to either side of him. 'Why have we turned down this track, Gisburne? It might get us there quicker, but it's far too narrow to travel in safety—this *is* Sherwood you know. Much better to stay in the open.'

'I have my reasons, my Lord.'

'Reasons?' The abbot reined in his horse as the track widened a fraction, so that Gisburne could ride next to him. Lowering his voice, he muttered, 'Gisburne, do you mean what I think you mean?'

'My Lord Abbot, I...'

Hugo cut across his companion. 'Gisburne, if my brother has told you to ensure that the Fairfax lands come to us today, then you can think again.'

'The sheriff was clear with his intentions. I ought to…'

Hugo growled, 'You ought to use that brain of yours!' He glanced around anxiously, before speaking more quietly. 'Do I need to remind you, Gisburne, that we are in the heart of Herne's domain—you have already meddled in the forest God's cave… I don't know what you've done this time, Gisburne, but you'd be a fool to invoke the wrath of the forest.'

'Herne is gone! I told you.'

Despairing, once again, of Gisburne's inability to learn from his previous mistakes, and only just managing not to remind him of the last time he'd tried to seek Herne's demise had sent him to the brink of madness, the abbot shivered. 'The Lord of the Trees is ancient—he doesn't just die.'

Wrinkling his nose, Gisburne sneered at his superior. 'Believe what you like, but removing one unpleasant nobleman from the world is hardly going to annoy a god, alive or dead.'

'You will *not* kill him, Gisburne.'

The trees around them began to rustle their leaves as Gisburne protested. 'But the Sheriff…'

Hugo gripped his reins as he watched the movement of the treetops above them. 'My brother doesn't always know what's good for him—and the forest… can't you feel it? It's not right today… Ride with Fairfax to his lands, befriend him—keep him on our side—but *don't* kill him—at least, not yet… The road forks towards the abbey soon. Before I take my leave, Gisburne, you will tell me *exactly* how you came to find Herne's cave in the first place…'

Abbot Hugo felt every muscle in his body tense. Each step his horse had taken towards the manor house ahead had only served to churn his stomach further. He hadn't liked what Gisburne had told him.

But then, when do I ever like what Gisburne says?

At last, as the late afternoon merged into evening, the entourage reached a wider lane and the bend in the road that led to his abbey. Without ceremony, he drew his men to a halt and called over his shoulder. 'Lord Fairfax, the road to St Mary's is nearby. I must bid you farewell. Gisburne will escort you to your lands before returning to Nottingham.'

'Thank you.' Peter bowed his head in gratitude. 'I'll be glad of his company. Safe ride, my Lord Abbot.'

'God go with you, Lord Fairfax.'

Watching Gisburne and his men lead Peter towards his home, Abbot Hugo muttered to himself. 'Soooo, Herne is dead, is he? Hmmm… I must go back to Nottingham and talk to Robert. If Herne really is gone, then Robin Hood will be at his weakest. Without his God to guide him, he's just an ordinary man with a sword…' He was already circling his horse back the way they'd come when he commanded, 'Captain, turn the men around…'

Marion gripped hold of the branch above her head to help steady her footing. From her position at the top of the old oak tree in which she crouched, she could hear horses approaching. A second later she saw what she'd been listening for.

'Robin! The abbot's coming back.'

Rushing to the base of the tree to join Tuck and Will, Robin called upwards, 'Just Hugo? Not Gisburne?'

'The abbot and three soldiers. Could we capture Hugo to see what he knows about the man from your premonition, Robin? I bet Gisburne will have told him about finding Herne's cave.'

Robin asked, 'Everyone agreed?'

Speaking in unison, Will and Tuck smiled at each other. 'Yes, Robin. Of course.'

'Then let's get ready. Roadside ambush positions.'

As the outlaws dived undercover on either side of the road, Marion whispered to Robin, 'You were going to suggest capturing Hugo, anyway, weren't you?'

'Well… it might have crossed my mind.'

The sound of the horses Marion had seen grew louder. Robin drew Albion from his belt, mumbling, 'Here we go again…,' before shouting at the top of his voice, 'Forward!'

Will Scarlet pushed Hugo towards the campfire. 'Stop complaining, my *Lord* Abbot. If you didn't want to be taken prisoner, you shouldn't make it so easy for us.'

Watching their unwilling guest struggling slightly as he tried and failed to free his tied wrists, Marion shook her head. 'Only three guards! What were you thinking?'

'I was in a hurry, and...' He rubbed his wrists together again, moaning, 'Did you have to tie my hands together so tightly?'

Will pushed his charge to the floor by the fire. 'Yeah.'

Standing next to Hugo, Robin regarded the sheriff's brother. 'You said you were in a hurry. *Why* were you in a hurry, Abbot?'

'None of your business, Wolfshead.'

'I think I...' Robin gestured to his companions. 'Sorry, I think *we* should be the judge of that.'

Tuck added a new log to the fire. As the outlaws sat next to the blaze, they watched the flames leap and crackle while the abbot protested.

'Just because you *think* you run the forest, it doesn't mean that you...'

Not interested in Abbot Hugo's opinion of him, Robin interrupted. 'Tell me how Gisburne found Herne's cave.'

'I have no idea what you're talking about.'

'I could get Will to ask you if you'd prefer?'

Hugo immediately inched nearer to the fire to put more space between himself and Will Scarlet. 'NO! That man's an animal.'

'Oi!'

Robin grinned at Will. 'Oh dear. Now you've

hurt his feelings, Abbot. And you know how animals can just randomly attack when they're angry? I mean, I'd have no control over him…'

Knowing he was beaten, Abbot Hugo sighed. 'Gisburne claims it was an accident—he'd been chasing a boy who'd been poaching. The boy ran into the cave. Gisburne lost him in the tunnels, but he did find Herne. Dead.'

For the first time that day, Will felt genuinely concerned. 'Dead?! Herne's not dead—is 'e Robin?'

CHAPTER SIX

'Father Harold you say?'

Nasir spotted the subtle flicker of a shared l(
between the brothers before Henry went on.

'I can't say we've seen him for some time.'

'We've no *need* to see him. The manor has its o(
chapel and chaplain.' Aidan took a sip of ale, bef(
spitting it out onto the floor, his face contorted
disgust. 'You call this ale *refreshment*, do you?'

John's hand was at Aidan's throat in seco(
'This is the best ale they can make. Without it, t
people...' Gritting his teeth, he took no notic
the strangled spluttering coming from his car
'...these people who toil long and hard for
father, the sheriff, every single day of their
with no reward... well... they would have n(
to drink beyond the water they gather in
barrels.'

A warning glance from Nasir stopped Henry om interfering.

Aidan's face had started to go red, but John adn't finished.

'You come in here demanding claret you know the tavern does not serve, you break pots in the market, throw stalls to the ground, tease people, and act like spoilt children. You are bullies and thieves. And *we* would like to know why you use your status to cause such mischief and suffering.'

Dropping Aidan's throat, John's eyes narrowed as the nobleman coughed and spluttered. 'Well?'

'We don't answer to the likes of you!' Henry leapt to his feet. 'You aren't even from Hathersage. I'd advise you to get out of here before my father hears about this and has you thrown into the midden!'

Much blurted out, 'Little John was *born* in Hathersage, he was. He knew you when you was both small!'

Henry and Aidan swapped another glance, before a knowing smile gradually crossed Henry's face.

'Little John, is it? Well now, I suggest you really do get out of town—*now*. Well, fancy that. John Little.' He paused, before adding, 'You *were*, John Little, weren't you?'

Cursing Much's naivety at giving him away, as well as his own lack of foresight, knowing he should have warned Much not to use his name, John moved forwards, towering over the two noblemen. 'Yes, I'm John Little, and I do remember you. You were overprivileged tiresome children when I lived here, and you haven't changed.'

'And *you* are an outlaw. A criminal. A Wolfshead!' Aidan shouted, creating a new wave of muted disquiet across the inn. 'And I could have you arrested at once.'

Amazed at how calm he was managing to keep, John addressed both Aidan, Henry, and the tavern as a whole at once. 'No, you couldn't. I'm not an outlaw in Hathersage. Anyway, I'm only a criminal in the eyes of a corrupt law and I would never hurt a soul on purpose—not like you two, who find sport in every cruel thing you do.'

Aidan abruptly pushed past Nasir and beckoned to Henry. 'Come, brother, we have heard enough.'

Henry followed. 'I think our Father—the *sheriff*—needs to be told that three of Robin Hood's men are in Hathersage.'

'Talking of fathers.' Getting up to bar their way, John said, 'Where is Father Harold?'

'What do you care of that meddling priest?'

John darted a warning glance at Much, hoping he'd understand that he didn't want them to know that Harold was his uncle. 'He is an innocent man who's gone missing, isn't that reason enough to care about his safety?'

Henry snorted. 'Who would have thought that the famous Little John could be so weak? Leaving his precious Sherwood Forest to chase about England after a single priest—and an interfering one at that.' He shoved John in the stomach and, with Aidan on his heels, strode away.

They'd reached the door before Lord Henry shouted back towards the outlaws. 'If you are not out of Hathersage by midnight, I'll summon my father's men.'

'I'm sorry John.'

'It's alright Much, I know you are.' John rested his back against a tree trunk at the side of a sheep field, wondering how many more times his friend was going to apologise.

'I shouldn't have given your name away, but...'

'Much, really—it's alright.' John tried not to

yawn. It had already been a long day, and it wasn't over yet. 'Let's just listen out for Nasir.'

'Do you think we'll hear him?'

'We will if we're quiet, Much.'

'Oh, yeah—sorry.' The young outlaw crouched to the ground and made a play of listening for the bird call that would tell them Nasir had discovered where the two noblemen had gone.

After a few minutes of hearing the bleat of the sheep in the fields around them, John said, 'It's enough to make me homesick.'

'Homesick? But there's no sheep in Sherwood, well, not many anyway.'

'I meant homesick for here. For when I was younger. Before Belleme made a slave of me, before Robin came to the forest.'

'Oh.' Much's forehead contracted into worry lines. 'You aren't going to stay here, are you? Once we find your uncle, I mean.'

Studying the roll of the hills, each spotted with white dots, just visible in the nighttime gloom, John became wistful. 'You heard the noblemen Much, I wouldn't be welcome back here.'

'But *they're* not good people. Thomas, *he's* good—he'd welcome you if you came back. I'm sure he would.'

John chuckled, 'I didn't think you wanted me to stay here.'

'I don't.' Much frowned again. 'I just don't want you not to be wanted here either.'

'Thank you, Much, but I couldn't leave Robin and the rest of you. You're my family now.'

'Uncle Harold is your family too.'

'He is—my last living relative—and, as he's a priest, they'll not be any more little Little's in my family; in Hathersage or anywhere.'

'Unless you and Meg have children.'

Knowing in his heart that Meg of Wickham would love to marry him and have a family, but also knowing that was unlikely to ever be a safe option for them, John simply said, 'I have to help him.'

'Course you do.' Much nodded emphatically. 'Cos, he's...'

The sound of a birdcall stopped Much's sentence in its tracks.

John jumped to his feet. 'Nasir.'

'It came from over there.' Much waved towards a path to their right.

'Then that's the way we're going to go.'

CHAPTER SEVEN

Silence coated the clearing. Even the outlaw's campfire held its breath for a second, before suddenly crackling louder, as if lending its weight to the argument against the Lord of the Tree's demise.

'What can you tell us about the nobleman you and Gisburne were with earlier, Hugo?'

'What?'

Tuck took a sip of ale before passing the flask around the group. 'You seem to be having trouble grasping simple questions, my Lord Abbot. Too much wine and not enough prayer, perhaps?'

'Alright, alright. His name is Peter Fairfax.'

'So, it *was* Peter…' Marion looked at the abbot. 'I wondered, but I wasn't sure.'

'The son of Lord and Lady Fairfax—the man and woman that *you* killed, wolfshead!' snapped Abbot Hugo.

'Me?' Robin exchanged an astonished glance with his friends. 'No, Abbot. I've killed no one that hasn't endangered my life or that of another. Why would you think I would harm the parents of a man I'd never heard of until today?'

On a signal from Robin, Tuck undid the abbot's bound arms. 'Here. Have some wine, Abbot. Perhaps it will help you see things more clearly.'

'Oh, thank you, Friar.' Flexing his wrists for a second, Hugo took a glug of the ale, grimacing at the taste. As he wiped a hand over his mouth, he looked up at Robin. 'So, you're claiming you did *not* kill a man and a woman as they travelled to Nottingham.'

Scarlet snapped, 'Your sort might kill for no reason. *We* do not.'

'Will is right, Abbot. *We* never kill for the sake of it.' Robin watched the dance of the flames while he waited for their prisoner to respond.

'Then why would Peter Fairfax say you did?'

'Because *he* is the man who attacked the cart, and I'm easy to blame.'

Taking refuge in his drink, the abbot found himself remembering how unstably Peter had acted while they'd dined at the castle. 'He killed his parents? Peter did? Are you certain?'

'If I wanted to accuse someone of a murder to clear my own name, I'd pick Gisburne.'

Hugo snorted. 'That I believe.' He lapsed into thoughtfulness for a while, before adding, 'Ummm… the Fairfax lands are due to go to my brother and I, if Peter dies.'

'Are they now?' Tuck couldn't keep his disapproval from his voice.

'Yes, they are. And it's no business of yours.'

Observing the abbot closely, Marion crossed her arms. 'I know that look, Abbot Hugo—you've thought of something.'

'I…'

Robin tossed a stray twig onto the fire. 'Let me guess, here I am telling you that Peter Fairfax is a murderer, and suddenly you see a reason to have him arrested…'

Marion took over. 'Meaning that his lands, if he were to hang for his parents' murders, would go to you and the sheriff.'

'I won't deny that.' Abbot Hugo's manner became conspiratorial. 'You could let me go and then capture Peter Fairfax *for* me. Bringing him back here, so I can take him to Nottingham for my brother to arrest.'

Will couldn't believe the cleric's nerve. 'Oh,

could we? Your servants, are we? You forget. You are *our* prisoner.'

Tuck glared at his fellow cleric in disgust. 'He just wants to get his greedy fingers on the Fairfax lands.'

The abbot, however, felt secure in his argument. 'Legally, as per his father's wishes, they'll come to me and Robert anyway.'

'But, if either of them survived…' Marion switched her attention from Robin to Abbot Hugo, '…the lands are still theirs. Not yours.'

'Peter said they were dead.'

Marion frowned. 'And Robin saw a vision of this, but—sometimes—visions can be a foreshadowing, or an alternate view. We've found that before.'

The abbot waved a dismissive hand. 'Yes, yes… but I don't believe that they survived. My brother would have heard about the attack from *them*, if that was the case. Don't you listen?'

'We even understood what you said.' Will's eyes narrowed as he moved, pressing the side of his body against the abbot. 'We just don't believe you're right, that's all.'

Trying to pretend he didn't feel threatened by the outlaw next to him, Hugo de Rainault flapped away their concerns. 'If you help me by capturing Peter Fairfax, I will allow you access to St. Mary's bountiful gardens and well-stocked larder for a month.'

'The abbey garden! That's a cook's paradise!' Friar Tuck's mouth dropped open. He could already taste the delicious meals he could prepare for the local community—not to mention for his fellow outlaws after a hard day in the forest.

Marion smiled as she saw Tuck looking longingly towards his cooking pot in anticipation of treats to come. 'A month's worth of food to share amongst the villagers.'

Pulling himself from daydreams of flavoursome stews and wholesome pies, Friar Tuck pointed a podgy finger at their guest. 'Swear on your faith, Abbot; swear that you will honour this promise!'

'I swear.'

Scarlet chuckled as he saw Tuck's determined expression. 'Look at you, already salivating at the thought of that garden!'

Considering the deal done, Abbot Hugo swivelled around so he didn't have to look at Will Scarlet. 'Tell me, Marion, what makes you believe the Fairfaxes are alive?'

'Oh, I have no idea whether they are or not. I just hope, for Peter's sake, that Robin's vision wasn't set in stone.'

'And do you think so, outlaw?' Hugo set his piercing eyes on Robin. 'Do you think the Fairfaxes might not be dead? That Peter may have only wounded them? It seems far-fetched to me. What say you?'

'That doesn't matter.' Robin mumbled as he replayed the Huntress's vision through his head once more. 'If you'll excuse me Abbot, I need to talk to my friends, in private.'

Will lingered at the abbot's side as Robin, Marion and Tuck moved away to stand under the branches of a wide oak tree, just out of their prisoner's hearing. Taking his dagger from his belt, Will played it through his fingers, watching the abbot's eyes widen in fear. Only when Robin beckoned him forwards did Will move, taking immense satisfaction from hearing the abbot's audible sigh of relief as he left his side.

Marion grinned, 'You enjoyed making Hugo think you were going to stay next to him didn't you, Will.'

'Very much.' Will Scarlet pushed his dagger back into his belt. 'So, what do you think, Robin?'

'Hugo's uneasy—I bet he's wondering if Gisburne lied about finding Herne's cave.'

'He seems quite keen to help us.' Friar Tuck piped up.

Marion followed Tuck's eyeline, watching as the abbot stared moodily into the fire. 'He just wants the Fairfax lands.'

'You're right, Little Flower. But Hugo is willing to help us—even if it's just to show up Gisburne—and then, for a month, we'll eat like kings!'

'But how are we supposed to capture Peter Fairfax?'

'Drag him out of his home.' Will grinned. 'By *his* hair, this time, Marion.'

'As much as I disliked him as a child, if we do that, then word will spread that we're attacking nobility in their homes. We don't want that sort of reputation.'

'I don't mind.'

'I know you don't, Will.' Marion shook her head. 'But Sherwood's our home. We protect that. We serve our motto. Or we're no better than common bandits.'

'Then how do we lure him here, to capture him?' Tuck, determined not to lose his chance to cook with the abbey's prime, homegrown ingredients, suggested, 'Maybe we can make the abbot help us?'

Robin leant against the nearest tree trunk and smiled. 'I've been thinking about that. I think he should write this Peter Fairfax a letter—an invitation to hunt in Sherwood.'

Will nodded slowly. 'And then the hunter becomes the hunted.'

The cave echoed with the rippling of water as the Huntress rotated a long stick around the pool before her. With each cycle, her concentration focused deeper, her mind clearing of all but the mission in hand.

Stirring more slowly now, she murmured softly, 'Come into view, Herne's Son, come into... ahhh... there you are.'

As the water cleared and the subject of her thoughts came into view, she stopped stirring. Resting her weight upon the stick, she stepped backwards and waited as the puddle bubbled around the edges of the vision.

'Thank you, Lord of the Trees. Ahh, so he does my bidding... Soon it will be time... tomorrow... it will happen tomorrow...'

CHAPTER EIGHT

Tomorrow… it will happen tomorrow…

Little John looked round, searching for the origin of the voice. There was no one there.

He massaged at his temples as he heard it again…

Tomorrow… it will happen tomorrow…

It was so faint, so far away, and yet so clear—so definite. *Did I hear it out loud or just in my head?*

John stayed perfectly still as he crouched next to Nasir and Much, observing the scene before them. Neither of them had moved. *They didn't hear anything…*

Was that Herne? It didn't sound like him… but… is this how Robin feels when Herne speaks to him?

John closed his eyes and counted to three before opening them again.

I'm just tired. Hearing things. Herne only helps Robin.

John forced himself to concentrate on the terrain before them. Since Nasir had signalled to Much and himself, he knew they were waiting for his instruction—for him to lead the way.

Herne, if that is you, I could do with all the help you can spare.

'That's the old charcoal burner's hut.' John could just make out the outline of the small dark building out against the fading light. 'It went out of use years back. I can't believe it's not fallen apart.'

Nasir kept his eyes on the small dwelling on the edge of the last field in the row. 'It is useful to someone.'

'And you watched Henry and Aidan go in there before you called us, Nasir?' Much muttered.

'No. An old man. Tall. Like John.'

Little John stood up, resting his weight on his quarterstaff. 'My uncle is in there?'

'I think so. He was dressed like a priest.'

'Has anyone else gone in?'

Nasir shook his head.

'Ow about them nobles?' Much asked.

Nasir pointed to a pathway running behind the hut, towards the right. 'They went past the hut. I was about to follow, when the priest came.'

'That's the path to De Grange Manor. Aidan

and Henry must have seen sense and gone home.' Hoping they'd only gone home to sleep rather than gone home to summon their father's guard, John observed the hut. 'But you think my uncle is in there… hmmm…' He stepped forwards. 'Come on you two, it's time you met my uncle.'

'But if he's in there, he can't be missing.' Much hurried after John. 'Thomas said he was missing.'

'So he did Much. So he did.'

'Do my eyes deceive me? John, is that you, my boy?'

'Uncle Harold.' John fought his instinctive desire to run forward and embrace his relative. Instead he stood his ground as he took in their surroundings.

The hut, only just big enough for the four of them if they didn't move around, smelt of musty neglect. Yet, there was evidence that a fire had been recently lit, and a chair and table to one side looked relatively clean and held a fresh candle.

'What are you doing here, Uncle?'

'I could ask you the same, my boy.' The priest cast a wary eye over his nephew's companions. 'Are you going to introduce me?'

'Nasir, Much, this is Father Harold Little.' John waved a hand towards his kin. 'Uncle, these are my friends.'

'Friends and fellow outlaws?'

'Does that matter?' John grasped his staff a little tighter.

'Not one bit.' Father Harold's face broke into a beam. 'No need to look so worried, I'm not about to beat you for not being able to recite the Lord's Prayer.'

'You did once. My backside was sore for a week.'

'Nonsense—only two days, I'm sure.' The priest chuckled. 'Anyway, that was your Pa—he'd have tanned your hide for far longer if I hadn't stepped in. He was a stickler for discipline.'

'No need to tell me that.' John rubbed his backside as if in sympathy with his childhood self.

'My brother, alas, was a tyrant.'

A shadow crossed John's face. 'That he was. I could never do anything right.'

Much was surprised. 'I always thought you were happy here. You often talk about Hathersage.'

'That's because I love the place—but my father...' John shuddered. '...every family has one rotten soul inside it, isn't that what you used to say, Uncle?'

'Did you? Is that true?' Much looked horrified as he turned to the priest. 'I only ever had my parents and Robin. Robin's not rotten. One of my parents weren't rotten, was they?'

'I'm sure they weren't, young man.'

'Oh, that's alright then.' Bouncing back instantly, Much said, 'We thought the nobles had got you?'

'What? All of them?' The priest chuckled again, until he saw the serious expression on his nephew's face. 'I assume you mean De Grange's offspring?'

'Henry and Aidan.' John noticed a fresh candle on the table. 'That looks like a church candle. It's of too good a quality for a villager or the townsfolk to own.'

'Aye, it is a church candle. One of mine.'

'You work in here?' Nasir took a small step nearer to the recently laid fire.

'No, but I like to help those too poor to have a few basic things—light and heat being the most basic of all.'

'With the exception of food and drink, perhaps?'

'Aye, you're right about that, John. I help with that when I can.' Father Harold swept an eye around the tiny hut. 'Been many a year since this place had a charcoal burner living in it.'

'So who lives 'ere now then?' Much asked.

'No one. Sometimes a passing vagrant stays, but mostly it's empty.' The priest tugged his cloak more firmly around his shoulders. 'You can feel the damp seeping from the very walls, can't you.'

'So, why are *you* here, Uncle?'

'I just told you—I like to help out. If a passing vagrant or beggar should happen by, then they'll find a candle and a fire ready to be lit.' Father Harold shrugged, 'I've been dropping by to put in a new candle and fire kindling like this for years. You can ask anyone.'

'And Aidan and Henry De Grange? Where do they come into things here?'

'Here? They don't. I can't imagine them ever setting foot in a place like this.'

John felt a tingle of unease that years of living in Sherwood had taught him to listen to. A sixth sense that told him his uncle was being economical with the truth. 'Nasir, Much... can you check outside, please? Make sure our two noble villains really have gone home and aren't sniffing around the countryside.'

Once the two outlaws left to make sure no trouble was approaching, John gave voice to the suspicion forming in his mind. 'Thomas the potter came all the way to Sherwood to find me because he thought you had gone missing. But you aren't missing, are you. I want to know what's going on. Now.'

'Where would you like me to start?'

'The beginning is the usual place, Uncle.'

'Indeed.' Father Harold reached for a piece of wood off the kindling pile he'd so recently put into place and added it to the fire. 'We might as well light this, it'll keep us warm.'

'No.' John put his hand out to stop him. 'Someone will see the smoke.'

Regarding his nephew with renewed respect, the priest put down the kindling. 'I see. And it would not be a good idea for many people to know you are here, am I right?'

'You are.' John said, 'Perhaps we should go to your church.'

'I think not.'

'Ah… because it would not be a good idea for people to know you are there?'

'I see we understand each other, John.'

Resting his weight on his quarterstaff, 'I wouldn't say that.'

'The noblemen men you mention are not happy with me. I like to be where they cannot find me.' The priest levelled his piercing grey gaze on John. 'You are here because Thomas came for you.'

'Obviously.' Little John felt his patience slipping. 'Uncle, please, we've travelled a long way. We are needed in Sherwood, but Thomas said you were in trouble, and so I came.'

'And I am grateful.'

A slow realisation came over the outlaw. '*You* asked Thomas to come and get me, didn't you? You aren't in trouble at all.'

'I admit it, yes, I did.' Father Harold sat on the only seat.

'Why not tell the truth? I would have come anyway.'

'We thought you wouldn't leave Sherwood for the real reason—but you might for a family member in trouble—and as I'm the only one left…'

'No wonder Thomas couldn't meet my eye when we went to the pottery.' John crossed his arms over his chest. 'And Thomas agreed to come all the way to Nottinghamshire because, why? The *real* reason. Now.'

'The lords Aidan and Henry broke into his pottery. Damaged over half of his stock because they felt like it. They were bored, apparently. I can still hear their laughter as they gloated about it in the tavern afterwards.'

'They should be arrested.'

'Yes, they should. But their father is the sheriff, and he shows no inclination to arrest his own sons. They see themselves as untouchable.'

'And you wanted my help.'

'Yes, and in doing so incurred their wrath.'

John's eyes flashed. 'Did they hurt you?'

'Fear not, no. I'm merely avoid them when I can—I thought best to wait for you to arrive before I confronted them again.' The priest fidgeted with his cloak's fastening. 'I assumed you would all come—Robin Hood's fame proceeds him.'

Realisation hit John like a bucket of cold water. 'I see... It wasn't me you wanted at all... you used me to bring Robin to you.'

Seeing he'd hurt his nephew's feelings, Harold quickly said, 'I'm sorry, John, I didn't mean...'

John cut through the explanation. 'Why did you want Robin?'

'I've tried everything else to tame those boys—to make them see their actions are wrong. And I've failed. I thought... maybe, if they were taught a lesson by an infamous outlaw...'

'And you didn't think *I* could do that without Robin?'

Father Harold got back to his feet, 'Now come on, John, don't take it personally. These men are arrogant and headstrong, they take no notice of their father, the church, or anyone. It's a miracle that they've not killed anyone yet.'

'You thought Robin was the only one who could show them the error of their ways?'

'Not the only one.' The priest spoke fast, as he saw John's expression darken further. 'I thought it worth a try.'

'Then why did Thomas let me think it was me you wanted? Why not simply ask for Robin to come?'

'Ahh.' The priest looked down at his feet. 'He... he was going to, but he told me it was you he saw first, and you just... assumed it was you we wanted to come and help us.'

John's shoulders slouched forwards. 'Of course... I'm such a fool. As if anyone would want my help over Robin's.'

'John, it wasn't...'

'Don't tell me it wasn't like that, Uncle. It's bad enough to know I'm considered as second best— unless it's worse than that! Perhaps you'd rather Will Scarlet was here? Or Friar Tuck maybe!'

'Nephew! Please... calm yourself. It wasn't like that at all. I was looking forward to seeing you.'

Hurt shattered John's normally placid temper as

he barked, 'If you'd wanted Robin, you should have had Thomas ask for him.'

'We thought you did everything together.'

'So did I…' John deflated as he confronted his uncle. 'Now that we both know differently, do you want me to go away again, or do you think Nasir, Much and I are good enough to help you?'

'Don't say it like that, John. I didn't mean to imply you weren't up to the task, it's just…'

'I know. Robin Hood is the famous outlaw. I'm going.' John turned on his heels and stormed out of the hut.

Much wanted to chase after John the second he saw his friend race out of the hut, his face like thunder, but Nasir stopped him.

'He needs time.'

'Ow do you know?'

'I know him. He will need us in a while, but now, he should be alone.'

Much glanced back towards the charcoal burner's hut. 'Should we go and ask the priest what happened?'

'You go. I'll keep watch.'

Much sprinted towards the hut, leaving the Saracen surveying the landscape. Waiting.

CHAPTER NINE

'It is time to come with us.'

John looked up at Nasir. He didn't bother to ask him how he'd found where he'd been sitting in the darkest part of a small cluster of trees. 'To where?'

'Your uncle has been living in a barn, John.' Much hopped anxiously from one foot to the other. 'We need to go there. It'll be warmer and there's food.'

'You two go, if you like.'

Much looked helplessly at Nasir, who gave him a dip of encouragement to go on. 'Your Uncle told us what happened. He *does* want your help, John—he don't think you're second best at all.'

'He's bound to say that, though.' John gave a heavy sigh. 'And he's right anyway. Robin would have thought of a way to help on the spot, but I can't think of a plan. Nothing.'

'Maybe we could think of something together?'

Seeing the gleam in Much's eyes, helpless in the face of his young friend's eagerness, John ruffled the top of his head. 'Aye, alright. We'll try—at least it'll be warmer in the barn.' He got up, 'But if we can't think of anything, we're going back to Sherwood tomorrow. Agreed?'

'Agreed.'

The barn was warm and comfortable. They sat in the centre, hidden from view by stacks of straw which had been stored there the previous harvest season, ready to feed the animals when winter came.

'Ow long has you been hiding in here?' Much made himself comfortable in a hollow of straw as Father Harold passed him a bowl of pottage.

'A week now.'

'Why?' John asked.

'Ah, well…'

'Ah well, *what?*'

'Like I started to explain before… I heard that Robin Hood liked to help churchmen, so I thought… I thought, if I went missing then he might come and…'

'And he'd come to rescue you and in the process sort out the sheriff's sons.' John stood up, his shaggy mane of hair hiding his face as he edged out towards the outside world. 'We could do that—Much, Nasir and me—but you'd prefer it if Robin was the one to save the day. That's twice you've made that very clear.'

'Where are you going, John?'

Much's enquiry met with no reply, as the barn door slammed shut. 'Why's he gone off again, Nasir? We said we'd try to think of a plan—we ain't even begun thinking yet.'

'He's hurting.' Father Harold clasped his hands together as if he was entreating divine inspiration. 'I've wounded his pride. Again. I didn't mean to. I was clumsy.'

Nasir observed the priest. 'Your nephew is a good man. He has saved many lives.'

'Yeah.' Much tipped some of his pottage down his throat. 'Robin'll be really missing his help.'

Father Harold clambered to his feet. 'I'm sure he is missing all of you. I'm sorry.' He hesitated before asking, 'Tell me about John, what's he been doing since he arrived in Sherwood?'

John knew he shouldn't be so angry—and that made him angrier. Looking up at the moon, he found himself wondering what Robin, Will, Marion and Tuck were doing.

Whatever it is, I bet they're helping someone. And I bet Robin knows exactly what to do.

Having returned to the crossroads, so he could watch the charcoal burner's hut to one side and the road towards the manor house on the other, John grumbled, 'If Robin needs help he has Herne to guide him. Who do I have? I must have been imagining that voice earlier.'

Beginning to wish he'd eaten some of the food his uncle had offered to them in his makeshift hideaway, John was about to get to his feet when he heard the voice again; faint, far away and unworldly.

Soon it will be time... tomorrow...

He spun around, but there was no one there.

'Herne? Is that you? Could you be a bit clearer with your instructions? I'm not Robin!' He shook his head, making himself listen to the nagging feeling in his gut telling him it wasn't the Lord of the Trees who he'd been hearing—but it was real. He wasn't imagining things.

'No, it didn't sound like Herne before, and it doesn't now. It's female... and yet...'

It will happen tomorrow...

John peered up into the canopy of the trees in which he stood. 'Tomorrow? What is going to happen tomorrow? And do I have to come up with a plan to make whatever it is work?'

The outlaws had been hiding in the forest along the edge of the road to Nottingham Castle since early morning. They watched and waited, listening to the birds overhead sing the day into life.

As the morning crept towards midday, Tuck stood up from where he'd been sitting at the foot of a tree. Craning forward a fraction, he finally saw what he'd been waiting for. Peter Fairfax was riding along the road.

Taking a silent step back, he gave a faint bird call.

A little further along the road, Marion jumped down from the tree in which she'd been acting as a lookout. 'That's Tuck. Peter must be getting close to—'

Will held up a hand. 'There. Look.'

'He's on his own.' Marion was surprised by the lack of an escort.

'Foolish.' Will snarled.

'Arrogant.' Marion muttered as Peter's horse approached closer, riding along the ever-narrowing road that would soon see him weaving through Sherwood itself.

Robin placed a hand on Marion's arm. 'He's not paying attention.'

A second later, Tuck joined them, brushing leaves from his cassock. He held a finger to his lips. 'Listen, Robin... I can hear...' He paused, straining to make out the voice of the man on the horse. 'Well, I never. He's talking to his horse. How strange.'

Will rolled his eyes, 'It will be if the horse answers back.'

Peter patted his horse's neck affectionately as he rode.

'They say this is a dangerous forest. Full of outlaws.' He scoffed in derision. 'Doesn't feel too dangerous to me. Does it to you, girl?'

Readjusting his reins, he relaxed into his saddle. 'I'm looking forward to the hunt. I think that simpering abbot and his stupid brother are going to be quite useful to me, not to mention...'

A rustle of movement in the trees broke through Peter's words. 'What was that?' Reining in his horse he shouted, 'Is anyone there? Show yourself!'

The silence that followed lasted for a few seconds—just long enough for Peter to relax. Then the outlaws leapt out of hiding, frightening the horse so that it reared.

'What the..?' Holding on tight, Peter struggled to control his mount while finding himself surrounded by four outlaws, each holding a drawn longbow, upon which four arrows were notched and aimed in his direction.

Robin kept his bow arm taught as he said, 'Lord Peter Fairfax. We've been waiting for you.'

'Waiting…'

Marion fixed her childhood tormentor with a steely stare. 'To take you to see Abbot Hugo—you were looking for him, weren't you, Peter.'

'Yes, but… how did you… who *are* you?'

'You know who we are—you certainly know who *I* am.' Robin cast his eyes over the nobleman with open curiosity. 'If you didn't, then you wouldn't have accused me of a crime you committed yourself.'

'I've done no such thing!'

He was the same as a child, Marion thought, *always denying what he'd done to avoid getting into trouble.* 'And you know who I am. Think back to when we were children.'

'I don't...' Peter's mouth dropped open. 'No. Marion? Marion of *Leaford*? Really? I haven't seen you since...'

Marion eased her bowstring back further as she finished his sentence for him '...your hands were full of my hair? Or since you kicked my shins until they bled?'

'A bully.' Will spoke through clenched teeth, his fists already itching to punch the man before them. 'I'm not a fan of bullies.'

Enjoying the flash of alarm that had fleetingly crossed Peter's face, Marion introduced him to her friend. 'This is Will Scarlet; he's going to lead your horse—and you—to our camp.'

Increasingly nervous and angry, Peter's eyes ranged from one outlaw to another. 'Your camp? I'm supposed to be going hunting. You've no right to...'

'Stop your whinging, Fairfax!' Will cut in as he lowered his bow and grabbed the horse's bridle. 'You've 'ad your hunt, it's just you were the prey for a change.'

CHAPTER TEN

Much wanted to ask John if he was alright, but he'd already asked him how he was three times, and three times he hadn't received an answer. Instead, Much said, 'I'm glad you came back.'

'Thank you, lad. I just needed to think, that's all.'

'What were you thinking about?' Much's innocent expression was troubled.

'I was wondering what Robin might do if he was here. I was also,' John fixed his gaze on his uncle, 'thinking that at least I now understand why, when we'd been told the local priest was missing, not one piece of gossip reached our ears about his disappearance when we were in the tavern. I knew something had bothered me last night—only now do I see what that was.'

'Ah…' Father John cast his eyes downwards, '…I admit it—we didn't want to alarm the whole town, so Thomas and I kept our plan to sort out the De Grange boys to ourselves.'

'Of course you did.' John could feel a sense of urgency prickling his palms. 'We need to act fast. I...'

'What is it?' Nasir fixed his shrewd eyes on John.

'There was a voice—like Herne, but not Herne. They said something was going to happen today, so I think we should be ready—expect something. Make a plan.'

Much asked. 'Is that why we're here? On the roadside?'

'It is.' John stepped out of their hiding place; one of the few patches of woodland that grew along the road next to an otherwise open terrain. He could just see the manor house in the far distance. 'I know I'm not Robin Hood, but I've finally got an idea anyway.'

'I'm sorry. I really am. I should not have got you here in the way I did—but, well, you are here now, and I'm sure your plan will be wonderful... you said you'd heard a voice?'

Frustrated by his uncle's sceptical tone, John wondered if this was how Robin felt every time someone questioned him about Herne's voice coming into his head. 'I did. Yes.'

'And after hearing it, you came up with a plan.'

'Eventually, yes.'

'Are you sure about this, John?' Father Harold flexed his elderly limbs.

Closing his eyes for a second, John struggled not to get cross. 'She said it would happen today.'

'I wish you'd tell me who 'she' is, John.' The priest persisted. 'And what exactly we are going to do when whatever is going to happen today actually happens.'

As John had no idea whose voice he'd heard (but was absolutely certain she was right about today being when they needed to act), he simply said, 'Uncle, if Robin Hood had said Herne had told him the situation would be sorted today, you'd believe him, wouldn't you.'

'I'm a priest, John... I don't believe in forest gods or...'

'I'd believe him.' Much said.

Nasir, who'd been observing John carefully, said, 'If you've been guided, we should wait until you know the time is right to act. And you *will* know.'

'Thank you, Nas.'

Hoping Nasir was right, John held his quarterstaff tightly, grateful for its reassuring familiarity. 'And you, Uncle, do you trust that we can help you?

Help Hathersage, without Will or Tuck or Marion? Without Robin?'

'I do. I'm sorry if I made you feel like I did not.'

'Right then,' John tensed as he heard the familiar sound of approaching horses from further down the road. 'That will be them—when they pass, we are going to the manor house.'

'We aren't going to stop the horses?'

'No, Much. We are going to let Lord Aidan and Lord Henry pass, then we'll go and speak to their father.' John crouched down in the undergrowth. 'Or to be more precise… you are, Uncle.'

'Me? We can't go into the manor; we'd be arrested on the spot.'

'Yeah. We would!' Much nodded profusely, 'I bet that Aidan and Henry told their father about us being here.'

The priest was unable to argue. 'I've spoken to his lordship before about his son's behaviour. He didn't believe me.'

'He will this time—eventually.'

'Why?'

'Because you are going to invite him to join us for a flagon of ale in the tavern. I think it's time the local sheriff heard the tales the people of Hathersage tell about his offspring, for himself.'

'He'd never come!'

'True, but this time you aren't going to talk to him about his sons. That's not why you're going.'

'It isn't?'

'No—you are going to tell him that that there are three outlaws in Hathersage—that one of them is your nephew, and you are going to have a drink with him—me—at the tavern later.'

'Aidan and Henry may have told him already.'

'True, but would he believe them?' John smiled, 'His sons have proved themselves unreliable once too often, I'd imagine—but you… if you and his sons had told him we were here, he might just stir himself to action.'

Much and Nasir shared a knowing glance as John went on.

'Tell me Uncle, do you have any changes of clothes in that barn of yours?'

Marion had observed her childhood tormentor closely as they'd led him through the forest. He'd been unusually quiet, but it was obvious from the range of ever-changing expressions that had crossed his face as they'd travelled, that he was battling a war between rage, indignation and fear. She'd found herself placing a palm on the handle of her dagger, just in case; his anger was not something that anyone should take lightly.

Now they'd arrived at the camp, she saw Peter draw his horse to an abrupt halt.

'Wait... stop a minute.' His voice wavered with shock, as if he hadn't believed the outlaws when they told him before who else they had at camp. 'That really *is* Abbot Hugo sitting over there!'

Will tutted. 'Observant, ain't he.'

Robin tapped a foot on the ground. 'Take a seat, Lord Fairfax.'

Peter looked down at the uneven forest floor. 'Here? But the abbot...'

'Is over there, yes. You will sit *here*.'

Peter looked anxiously at his mount. 'My horse—'

'—will be cared for. Now, dismount before I pull you down myself.'

As Peter obeyed Robin, and Will tethered the mare to a tree, Tuck indicated the nearby campfire. 'Ale?'

'Oh! Why, thank you... brother.'

Accepting a cup of ale, Peter took a small sip as

Will sat on his right side, and Tuck lowered himself down on his left.

Not bothering to hide his fear, Fairfax stuttered, 'Do you two have to sit so close to me?'

'I think we do, don't you, Will?' Tuck looked around their guest at Scarlet.

'Definitely.'

Feeling the warmth of the fire on his back, Robin enjoyed a private smile as he watched Tuck and Will unnerve their guest. 'Now then, Peter—you attacked two people in the forest. You blamed me—why?'

'I did no such...'

'You did.' Robin interrupted. 'So, why did you attack them? And why disguise yourself as an outlaw to do it?'

Looking at the bound figure of the abbot on the far side of the camp, and not knowing what fate lay in store for them both, was enough to make Peter confess. 'Oh, all right. I did. But I didn't *mean* to attack anyone. And—*obviously*—I dressed as an outlaw to keep myself safe from *actual* outlaws.'

Not convinced, Robin asked bluntly, 'The attack... Tell us about that...'

'If you insist.'

'We do.' Will extracted his knife from his belt. 'Talk.'

After taking another drink to steady his nerves, Peter gave an overly dramatic sigh. There seemed to be a slight change in his personality, as if he was disconnecting from what he was saying, bluntly. 'It's simple. I needed to speak with the people in the cart and I knew they would be on their way to Nottingham—although I wasn't sure when. I waited some time. I got quite cold.'

'Aww... bless 'im.' Will stabbed the tip of his blade into the ground between Peter's feet, making him flinch.

'Poor lad.' Tuck muttered sarcastically. 'The hardship! Fancy it getting cold in the forest!'

With a wry smile, Robin coaxed, 'So, you waited in the forest, then what?'

'I saw them coming...' Peter closed his eyes, the memory of the day crystal clear in his mind...

CHAPTER ELEVEN

A cart trundled along the forest road, its two occupants, sat side by side, were taking no heed of the forest around them.

Peter felt his stomach fizz with righteous indignation as he saw them approach, his long wait in the cold forest finally over.

No doubts assailed him. He'd planned this for so long, replaying how he'd ambush his parents again and again until, in his mind at least, there was nothing that could go wrong.

Drawing a longbow he'd purchased especially for the task ahead, Peter emerged from between the trees, the cold forgotten as he shouted, 'STOP YOUR CART AT ONCE!'

Obeying in alarm, making the elderly horse whinny at the rapid tugging of its reins, Lord Fairfax demanded, 'What is the meaning of this?'

Before he'd finished speaking however, an amazed Lady Fairfax had placed a trembling hand on her husband's arm. '*Peter?*'

The halted horse stamped a hoof restlessly as, ignoring his mother, Peter ordered, 'Get down from there—both of you. Now.'

Horrified, Lady Fairfax reached a hand towards her son. 'Peter. Why do you talk to us like this? When did you get back from France?'

Dismissing the offered palm, Peter sniped, 'Why would you care?'

'Because we're your parents!'

Disgusted by the film of tears forming in his mother's eyes, Peter yelled, 'You are not!'

'Alright, Peter.' With a consoling look at his wife, Lord Fairfax let go of the reins. 'I'm getting down... but please stop pointing that bow at your mother.'

'She is not my mother!'

'Don't be ridiculous, Peter!' Lord Fairfax studied his son in bewilderment. 'Now, what do you think you're doing?'

'Taking control of what's rightfully mine! Your home and land; they aren't yours at all.' Peter lowered his bow a fraction, but kept the arrow firmly notched in place. 'They belonged to my *real* father. That makes them mine now.'

Lady Fairfax stuttered, 'But... but your father's brother died so long ago. He asked us to raise you—you came to us willingly. You called us your parents. And now...'

Peter cut through his mother's desperate need to make him see sense. 'And now I've grown up! I've seen battle! I've heard story after story about young noblemen being cheated out of their rightful home and lands in their absence—that's *not* going to happen to me!'

'How dare you?' Lord Fairfax stood up straighter, moving nearer to his son. 'We would never...'

'Stay still!' Peter pulled his bowstring back. 'Don't come any closer or I'll shoot!'

'Peter... son... please...' Lady Fairfax's eyes widened in horror.

'Shut up!'

Taking no heed of the arrow aimed at his chest, Lord Fairfax took another step forward. Coaxingly calm, he beseeched, 'Lower that bow. There's no need for this! We love you, son, come on.'

'I SAID STAY STILL.'

Lord Fairfax froze, the final vestiges of colour draining from his face. 'Look, let's all turn round and go back to the manor and...'

Peter interrupted with a grunt. 'Where you're

surrounded by your loyal servants who will overpower me. I don't think so.'

From behind her husband, Lady Fairfax pleaded, 'Please Peter, this is madness...'

Again he cut across his mother. 'I've met someone—a Lady of the French Court. Her family won't agree to our marriage unless it is clear that the Fairfax lands are mine—in my *own* right.'

Lord Fairfax exchanged a worried glance with his wife as he tried again. 'But, son...'

'But nothing! I'm *not* your son.'

The arrow had fired before Peter had registered what was happening; Lady Fairfax's scream echoing around his skull as her husband slumped to the ground in a howl of pain, which soon subsided into sadness. 'Peter...'

As their adopted son's name died on her husband's lips, Lady Fairfax scrambled from the cart. 'No! Edmund!' Cradling her husband's fallen body, she stared at her son in wide-eyed disbelief, in a state of shock 'You shot him! You shot your father.'

'I didn't intend... No.' Peter's eyes were wide with horror. 'He was walking towards me.'

'You've killed him!!' she wailed.

Shaken, Peter muttered, 'I didn't intend to.' He glanced around, relieved to see no one else was in sight. 'He... he wouldn't listen. I just wanted him to listen.'

Tears flowed down Lady Fairfax's face. 'But you weren't making sense, son... and now...'

'I thought he was going to draw his sword. I thought...' Anger overtook Peter's moment of remorse, as his brain struggled to comprehend the scale of what he'd done, accidentally or not. He almost became a spoiled child, stamping his feet. 'Oh, this is SO typical! I'll pull the arrow out. He'll be fine.'

Lady Fairfax's cry of 'No, Peter. Leave him. PETER!!' came too late, for her son had already tugged the wooden shaft free and thrown it to the ground in disgust.

'How could he go and die?!' Peter's face reddened in angry frustration now. 'How dare he? I was just trying to...'

'Peter... stop.' Trying to protect the fallen body, Lady Fairfax pleaded, 'Get away from him. Give him his dignity.'

Suddenly sobbing, his fury giving way to confusion, unable to fathom how his plan had gone so badly wrong, Peter wailed, 'I just wanted you both gone from my lands—not killed. I was trying to scare you off.'

Horrified by the madness that had taken hold of Peter, as well as by what he'd done, Lady Fairfax stroked her husband's hair. 'But they're *our* lands. What right have you to…?'

Jumping to his feet, Peter threw down the bow and drew his sword, screaming, 'EVERY RIGHT!'

Lady Fairfax shook her head. 'All you had to do was wait! They'd have come to you in time.'

Sweat broke out on Peter's brow. 'But they were NEVER YOURS!'

A sudden fury gave Lady Fairfax the strength to jump to her feet, as she shouted, 'I'll have you brought before the sheriff for this!' Her whole being trembled as the shock of the situation overtook her, and her brow creased heavily in confusion. 'What can have happened to you in France?!'

'You will not bring me before anyone!' Panic rose in Peter's gut. 'It was an accident. It was nothing!'

'*Nothing?* You have murdered your father!'

His rage rushed back through him, overflowing the panic. 'I TOLD YOU! HE WAS *NOT* MY FATHER!'

'Then he acted like one to you. He brought you up.'

Peter waved his sword around in front of him as a riot of conflicting thoughts filled head.

Edging backwards, Lady Fairfax watched the glinting blade in horror. 'Put away your sword. Peter, I beseech you...'

'NOOOOOO!' The tip of the sword sank into Lady Fairfax's chest, as Peter gave a 'Hah!!' of triumph.

Clutching her hands to her bloody chest, Lady Fairfax screamed, 'No.... Peter... no...,' her knees folding as she hit the ground.

'You can now act like his wife.' Peter's breathing was laboured. 'Dead too.'

'Urgh... Peter... why?'

Watching without answering his mother's final question, Peter smiled as Lady Fairfax sank to the ground.

CHAPTER TWELVE

The outlaw's combined sense of disgust was palpable. No one had spoken while Lord Peter Fairfax had told his tale—each of them stunned by the callousness of the man sat by their campfire.

Perfectly calm, as if he'd done nothing more than tell them a bedtime story, Peter finished his tale. 'After she'd fallen to the ground I took the manor key from father's belt and went home.'

Friar Tuck wasn't sure he could believe what he was hearing. 'You just took his keys?'

'They were mine anyway.'

'But... Lady Fairfax...'

'It was her own fault... she goaded me. I do wish I hadn't killed them, but you all understand how it is, don't you? Everyone knows how you despise the way the rich have everything. I wanted what was mine—now I have it.'

Marion ran a hand through her hair, remembering just how much it had hurt when he'd pulled it as a child. 'You killed them for lands that would have come to you anyway?'

'Oh, come on!' Peter dismissed the look of horror on her face. 'I know you're sympathetic to my cause. You'd hardly live like this if you weren't killers yourselves. Especially you, Marion—you have had Leaford taken from you. You must understand.'

'I most certainly do not! I loved my father, I'd never have…'

'There you are, you see! It is all very straightforward really—they *weren't* my real parents.' With stoic resolve he continued. 'I've honoured my real father's wish to make a man of myself in battle, and now his lands will help me to create a life; now that my time fighting is over.'

Robin felt an icy chill wash over him in the face of Peter's madness. 'You killed a good man.'

'Don't you *listen*, outlaw?!' Fairfax's irritation seemed unhinged. 'I told you, I didn't mean to kill them, just to frighten them—things went wrong, but what's done is done, and the lands are mine.'

Tuck crossed himself as he muttered, 'Dear God.'

Struggling to comprehend what had been done, Marion asked, 'Peter, why would your French lady want anyone murdered, to get enough land to win her heart?'

'Yeah.' Will agreed. 'If she loved you, she'd be with you anyway.'

His face glowing a hot red, Peter barked, 'Of course she loves me! But... but...' In his frustration at their lack of understanding, he struggled to find the words. 'Even if she didn't, I'm still entitled to my lands! I *keep* telling you, those people were only my adopted parents. I'm the *real* Lord Fairfax.'

Standing up, Robin temporarily disregarded their guest while he spoke to his friends. 'Keep an eye on him. I'm going to talk to Hugo. I think he should know what the newest Lord Fairfax did to claim his lands.'

'No! I...'

Peter tried to get to his feet, but Will and Tuck grabbed an arm apiece and swiftly pulled him back in place.

'Oh no you don't.' Scarlet glared at him with contempt. 'You're not going anywhere. You're staying here.'

'You're hurting my arms.'

Tuck was unmoved by the complaint. 'We'll loosen our grip when you calm down.'

'Yeah, or we might have an accident. The sort of

accident that leaves you dead, just like the one you had with your parents.'

The murderous expression on Will's face made Robin rethink his plans. 'On second thoughts, I think the abbot should join us here.'

'That's him.' Father Harold waved towards a cart that was trundling along the road in their direction. 'He has never ridden well and prefers to travel in a cart.'

'Unusual for a sheriff.' Much muttered.

'He prefers that his deputy and captain of the guard do anything that means leaving the manor when it comes to getting his hands dirty, but when I told him some of Robin Hood's men had come to Hathersage because word had reached them of the behaviour of his sons, then he had to act. Personally.'

'Can you imagine what the king would have said if he got to hear that we'd been in Hathersage, and no one had tried to arrest us?' John grinned.

Father Harold gave his nephew a hearty slap on the back, 'Well done, John, I didn't think he'd listen to me—in fact, he said he didn't believe me—right up until I mentioned that Little John was here.'

'As he's coming to see us, we should do him the curtesy of providing him with a warm welcome.' John winked as he notched an arrow to his bow. 'How many guards?'

'Three.' Nasir turned to the priest. 'Will there be any in the cart?'

'He never has soldiers in with him, as far as I know. This isn't Sherwood.' The priest grimaced. 'But, as he knows you're here, there might be more.'

'I think we should assume there will be.' John gestured to the landscape at large. 'At least the ground is open—nowhere to hide additional soldiers.'

Nasir watched the cart with a practiced eye. 'I would say two or three extra men—it rides too low for just one passenger.'

John accepted the Saracen's prediction without question. 'I don't want to hurt the soldiers unless we've no choice. Much and Nasir, you know what to do. Uncle, I'd stay out of the way if I were you.'

The sun was going down behind the trees as Abbot Hugo was escorted from one side of the outlaw's camp to the other.

'Whilst I appreciate being allowed closer to the fire, when are you going to let me go, outlaw?'

Peter didn't wait until Hugo had sat down before he started to plead with the cleric. 'Make them let *me* go, abbot! They're accusing me of all sorts of things I didn't do!'

'Be quiet, Peter!' Marion had had just about enough of her childhood tormentor.

Robin signalled to the fireside 'Please, Abbot, sit down.'

Clumsily Hugo obeyed. 'What do you want of me, Wolfshead?'

'I want Lord Fairfax to be arrested for murder.'

'No!' barked Peter.

'Gladly.' Abbot Hugo replied.

Peter was stunned. 'No! Abbot—Hugo—how can you take the word of these scum!? They *are* murderers! There's no proof I've done anything!'

The abbot rounded on him, reminding everyone present that the younger De Rainault brother was no dolt, and they'd be stupid to ever forget that. 'Which is it to be, Peter—that you've done nothing—or that there is no *proof* that you've done *something*?'

Peter's forehead furrowed as he struggled to understand what the abbot was asking him. 'But Robin, Will, Tuck... *Marion*... you're outlaws! You *must* understand. Sometimes there are deaths... for the greater good... to...'

'There is *never* a death that can be claimed as a deed for the greater good.' Robin's anger was all the more powerful for the quietness of its delivery.

'Well, ummm...' The abbot mumbled, 'I can maybe think of one, but...' He risked a glance at Tuck, who mutely acknowledged his suggestion.

'Shut up, Abbot, you ain't helping.' Will was still struggling against the urge to punch Peter for hurting Marion all those years ago.

'Scarlet, untie the abbot's men.' Robin gestured to where the men-at-arms had been waiting, bound at the wrists and ankles, since being apprehended. 'They need to escort our prisoner to Nottingham.'

'Certainly. Be good to see the back of 'em.'

Tuck agreed. 'Yes, they're eating us out of pork like you wouldn't believe!'

Stunned that the outlaws bothered to feed their prisoners, Peter watched Will Scarlet, the most notorious of the outlaws, head off to free the soldiers, his incomprehension of the situation was written all over his face. He murmured to Tuck, 'Gisburne said you were thieves and murderers.'

'Gisburne is a fool.'

'I'm not going to Nottingham!' Searching desperately for a way out, Peter suddenly lunged forwards and grabbed Marion.

Letting out a shriek of anger, Marion kicked out sharply. 'Oh! Peter! Let go of me!'

'Ow!' Wincing slightly, Peter grinned. 'Still feisty then, Marion.'

As his hands came to her throat, Marion gasped for air. 'Get... off me...'

The other outlaws, the abbot, and his men froze as Peter manhandled Marion away from the fire.

'She's coming with me. To allow me safe passage out of here.'

'Oh, great!' Will groaned. *Here we go again!*

Tuck muttered out of the corner of his mouth. 'He's got no weapon.'

Scarlet sighed. 'He don't need one—he's been fighting in France—he could snap her neck in seconds. Believe me, I know.'

Robin's eyes never left Peter as he drew back his bow. 'Let my wife go. I don't want to shoot you.'

'Then don't.' Peter kept moving backwards, dragging Marion with him.

'Do you really want to die in the same way as your father?'

Enraged further, Peter's eyes shone with a dangerous zeal. 'He. Was. NOT MY FATHER!'

Robin remained composed as the breeze that had been rustling the leaves above them, blew a little harder, whistling through the branches. 'Let go of Marion, or I *will* shoot. Unlike you, I'm an excellent shot.'

As Robin eased his bowstring back another inch, Tuck spoke urgently. 'He really is Peter. He can shoot anything. Please let her go.'

Becoming more unstable by the second, Peter bellowed, 'Have her then!'; throwing Marion forwards with such force that she hit the ground.

'I'll run faster without—ahhh!' Peter found himself going nowhere, as Will Scarlet barrelled into his side, tackling him to the forest floor as the wind began to howl through the trees.

'You ain't going anywhere!'

Peter fought against Will's iron grasp. 'Let me go! LET ME GO!'

Ignoring Peter, knowing there was no way he could escape from Will, Robin ran to Marion's side.

'Are you alright?' He crouched down, cupping her face in his hands.

'Yes, I think so. He didn't leave with half my hair this time, at least!'

Helping her to her feet, checking for injuries, Robin frowned as he spotted some bruises developing on Marion's skin. 'No, but he's left a nasty mark round your neck. Let's get a wet cloth to soothe the...' Breaking off, Robin felt a familiar change to the air.

A figure appeared through the trees.

'Wait... it is...'

From his position on the sidelines of the action, Abbot Hugo gasped in fearful awe. 'Herne! The horned God!' He lowered his voice, muttering to himself, 'Gisburne, you are a lying fool! It lives.'

CHAPTER THIRTEEN

Peter Fairfax shook with fear. 'An apparition! This forest is cursed! I must not look at it. Must. Not. Look. At it. Let me leave!!'

Will gave him a slap across the face. 'Stop struggling, you idiot.'

'I will not look. You can't make me. Let go of me!'

Tuck kept his eyes fixed on the abbot. 'Herne has come to us.'

Hugo shook his head. 'That looks like no man. If this is your god, why does he look that way? What is it?'

Tuck turned to the being before Robin. 'Well, bless me, Abbot, you're right.'

Will, Tuck and Marion looked to their leader for an explanation, as they gathered around a frantic Peter.

'She's not Herne, no.' Robin gave their mystical visitor a polite bow. 'Huntress, you are welcome here.'

Raising her arms out to each side, reminding the outlaws of the Lord of the Trees once more, the Huntress focused on Robin. 'Herne was wise to trust in you, outlaw. I thank you for capturing this creature.'

As the Huntress twisted around to face Peter, he cowered further, his whole body dotting with perspiration as he trembled with fear.

'What is happening? I don't like it!'

Gripping the back of Peter's head, Will forced him to face the Huntress. 'Look at her, you coward!'

Peter closed his eyes. 'I will not!'

The Huntress's accusation rebounded around the camp. 'You killed your father and mortally wounded your mother. She was at the point of death.'

'I did not!' Fairfax's eyes flicked back open as he cried out in desperation. 'You have no proof. No one has proof!'

'*I* am proof!' The Huntress glided towards Peter, the flames of the fire leaping upwards, burning a deeper crimson as she moved. '*I* am witness! And Herne's Son is my instrument of justice.'

'But... I didn't... it was an accident... I didn't... I...' Peter's bluster faltered as he realised what the

113

Huntress had said. 'Wait… do you mean… Lady Fairfax lives?'

'She lives.'

Robin of Loxley smiled as he dropped to one knee before Herne's ally. 'Lady Fairfax, Herne's Huntress. It's an honour.'

'Lady Fairfax I was—Lady Fairfax I will be again, once the magic of the merciful Herne has finished healing me. You are a wise man to have worked out that we are one, outlaw. However, there is no need to bow before me.'

Marion knelt at Robin's side, the other outlaws following her lead. 'It is a sign of respect, my Lady. You are welcome here.'

The Huntress inclined her head in recognition of their deference, before lowering her arms to her sides. 'I beseech you all, get up off your knees now.'

Peter felt his own knees weaken as, with one arm still firmly within Scarlet's grasp, he struggled anew. 'This is madness! You can't be her. You can't be!'

'And yet I am… and you will go with the abbot to Nottingham, to face justice.'

'No! I refuse to believe any of this. LET GO!' With an immense burst of strength born of desperation, Peter freed himself from Will's hands.

'Hell! He's a slippery sod!'

Tuck shouted, 'He's got your sword, Scarlet. Stop him!'

Peter raised the stolen sword, flailing it out in front of him.

Marion shouted, 'Look out, Robin! He's heading for the Huntress.'

Diving forward, Robin bellowed, 'No, Peter! You've already hurt her enough!'

'She's a demon—she should be sent to hell! DIE!!' Peter lunged at his mother, but he was too slow—hitting Robin instead as the outlaw intercepted the assault.

'Arrghhh!' Sinking to the ground, Robin held a hand over his bleeding arm as Peter circled round and disappeared between the trees.

'Robin!' Marion rushed to his side as Will readied himself to give chase.

'He's getting away! Let's go!'

Robin clambered to his feet. 'No! I'll go.'

Marion shook her head. 'But you're bleeding... your arm...'

Abbot Hugo interrupted, 'My men should go! He should be arrested!'

'No! I SAID I'LL GO.' Robin began to run. He'd not got far before he called over his shoulder. 'Look after our guests.'

Annoyed, Will kicked at an exposed tree root. 'He's doing it again—off on his own. And wounded this time.'

Tuck shrugged. 'A leader has to lead, Scarlet.'

The Huntress glided towards them. 'You must let him do this. I have seen—he is the one who tries.'

'Tries?' Marion asked.

'You will see.'

'But his arm…'

'The Hooded Man will mend.'

Marion swallowed, 'But the path Peter has taken…'

Scarlet looked in the direction that Robin had taken. 'What about it?'

'The ground falls away—suddenly—without warning. He does not know the forest.'

'Of course…' Will glanced back towards the Huntress. 'Well, let's hope Robin catches him before he falls.'

The midday sun shone through the trees, the leaves filtering the rays, cooling the temperature beneath the forest's canopy. Robin, however, felt sticky sweat coat him as, a hand still clutching his wound, he sprinted as fast as he could. The pain that shot through him was forgotten as he pounded after Peter, desperate to catch up with him before it was too late.

Pushing himself to move faster still, he was finally rewarded with the sound of footsteps running ahead of him. Robin shouted as loud as he could. 'Peter!! There's a drop ahead! Peter!! Stop!'

The scream of panicked shock that came in answer to his warning told Robin he was too late.

A strangled, desperate voice rang from below. 'Wolfshead! You've got to help me.'

In pain and out of breath, Robin dashed to the quarry edge and peered down to see Peter hanging onto a ledge just out of reach. 'I'm not sure I can. It's not safe to put my weight on the edge too.'

'Don't try and climb down. Just pull me up. *Please.*'

Robin frantically searched around him for anything that he might be able to lower down to pull Peter up with. 'If you hadn't cut my arm open, it would be a lot easier.'

Paralysed with fear, Peter was almost sobbing. 'You can't just leave me hanging here!'

'You left your mother to bleed to death.'

'I thought she was dead.'

'Is that supposed to make it right?' Unable to find anything for Peter to grab hold off, Robin gingerly lay against the crumbling quarry edge.

His eyes wide with terror, Peter gulped. 'I really didn't mean any of this to happen.'

'Yet it's happened. And you must atone for that.' Robin wriggled closer to the edge, sprinkling a light rain of dusty rubble down onto Peter.

Peter coughed, blinking as his eyes filled with grit. 'Prove to me you're not what people say you are. A thief and a murderer.'

Inching forward once more, Robin tested the ground as he moved. 'I don't run in those circles, Peter. The people here know my truth.'

The sound of the roots Peter was holding onto slowly ripping out of the uneven quarry edge was drowned out by his cry of, 'It's tearing. Help me, Robin!'

'Grab hold.' Robin lunged forwards.

'But your arm…'

'Just grab hold!' Robin tried to steady himself, trying to deny the throbbing pain in his arm as he grabbed an exposed tree root to his side, hoping it was buried enough within the fractured ground to hold their combined weight.

With a nosy exhalation, Peter swung himself upwards, just managing to catch hold of Robin's offered hand.

'Tighter!' Sweat poured off Robin as he tried to haul Peter to safety, while trying to deny the agony that was shooting through his other arm. 'Come on, Peter. I need you to hold tighter.'

'I can't…'

Robin gritted his teeth. 'Yes… you… can…'

Gasping with pain as he heaved, Robin gradually hauled Peter to the surface, as a mix of earth and stone cracked and creaked under the strain. Until, with a final grunt of effort, they both fell back onto the firm forest floor.

An exhausted Peter stared at Herne's Son in wonder. 'I… I thought you'd let me drop.'

Robin wiped the sweat from his eyes with his sleeve. 'I told you; I'm not a killer.'

Still indignant, Peter shook some dust from his hair. 'You threatened to shoot me.'

'You had your arm around my wife's neck.'

'Yes… I did. I'm sorry.' Defeated and exhausted, Peter examined his grazed palms, looking at this as if they belonged to someone else. 'I was scared. And my head is always… it's seen so many bad things. I can't… I just can't… rid myself of them. One

minute I feel like I'm me. The next, I feel like...
I'm... I don't know. I can't explain it.'

'Come back to the camp. Say sorry to Marion.'

Peter wrapped his arms around himself, as he
rocked back and forth. '*She...* she might still be
there.'

'The Huntress has gone.'

'How do you know?'

Robin squeezed a hand around his injured arm
and winced. 'I just know.'

'But...' Peter's eyes filled with self-pitying tears.
'How was that—she—my...'

'I don't know how. But it was.' Running out of
sympathy, Robin mumbled. 'Hell, my arm hurts.'

'Sorry.'

Wincing as he flexed his injured limb, trying
to loosen the muscles that had locked while he was
dragging Peter to safety, Robin gently asked, 'What
happened to you? Every man is changed by war...
but not many turn on the people who love them.'

The young Lord Fairfax wiped the back of a
palm over his tear-stained face. 'I met a man in
France who'd known my father—my *real* father. He
was convinced he had been murdered for his lands.'

'And you believed him?'

'Why would he lie?'

'For entertainment—to enjoy seeing your reaction.'

Peter was horror struck. 'But...'

'Will occasionally tells stories of his life in battle. He's mentioned a few times that battlefields are either frightening or boring—men make up all sorts of things to fill the time. To amuse themselves— often at the expense of others.'

Not wanting to believe what Robin was saying, Peter shook his head angrily. 'No... no, my adopted father saw my real father dead. It's the only thing that makes sense.'

'Abbot Hugo told Marion that your real father died after a long illness.'

'Yes—but that's because he was poisoned. *They* poisoned him.'

'Do you truly believe that?'

Peter bit his lip and seemed to visibly start trembling. 'I don't know what to believe anymore. I just want this all to go away. The pain. The images in my head. I'm confused.'

Robin reached out his good arm to help Peter up. 'Tell me... is there really a lady in France waiting to hear from you?'

'No... she... she wasn't my idea. One of the men in my squad, they thought such a fable would be an excuse to ensure I got my lands—but things got out of hand.' He let out a low groan. 'I didn't want to share my home with the couple who'd robbed my father of his lands and life.'

'Peter, if you believed that your adopted parents killed for the family title, why didn't you seek the truth peacefully? Why didn't you go to the sheriff? The king even?'

Peter trembled more, as he admitted, 'I... I don't know.'

'Lord and Lady Fairfax... they loved you as a natural son.'

'Oh God... what have I done!' Sinking back to the ground in despair, Peter ran his hands over his face. 'My father—he wasn't poisoned—was he?'

'I doubt it very much.'

To Robin's astonishment, Peter rolled into a ball on the ground, tears streaming down his face, as he sobbed. 'Why did you rescue me? You should have let me drop... I didn't deserve to be rescued.'

Robin reached out his hand. 'Come back with me. It isn't too late. You still have so much to live for.' A wave of pain washed through him, causing him to gasp aloud. 'Despite this wound you're given me, I'll help you. *We'll* help you. All you need to do is ask.'

'Help me how?'

'By showing you can start again. You could have a new life as someone else.'

Peter's face was blotched with fatigue and tears. 'But the abbot is waiting to arrest me.'

'You can leave Hugo to us.' Robin paused before adding, 'Look Peter, this is your one chance to live as a free man—your punishment will be that you'll have no lands and money. You'd have to survive off your wits.'

'I wouldn't hang?'

'Come back to the camp. We can give you more suitable clothes, some food and water, and get you safely out of Sherwood. After that, it would be down to you.' Robin smiled. 'You could find peace somewhere else.'

Sitting up, Peter's face lit into an unaccustomed smile. 'Find peace? You really mean it? Peace of mind again? Somewhere quiet?'

'Yes. So, will you come with me?'

Peter's smile dimmed as he muttered, 'I really didn't mean to kill him. He... he was kind to me. I was never a good shot with a bow.'

Robin felt uneasy as the man before him looked as if he was about to cry again. 'Do you need some time to think?'

'Think? Yes… yes, I will think. See if my head clears of the clouds.'

Dipping his head in acknowledgment, Robin glanced towards the heart of Sherwood. 'I must go back. My arm needs bandaging. Follow the path back and you will find us when you are ready. Yes?'

'Yes. Thank you, Robin… I really don't deserve…'

'Everyone deserves a second chance, Peter.' Robin turned to walk back to the camp. 'Everyone.'

'Oh!' Robin winced as Marion whacked a palm hard against his good arm.

'Don't you *ever* do that again! That arm needed tending to *before* you went racing off.'

'If I hadn't gone, he'd have ended up at the bottom of the quarry. The fall would have killed him'

As Marion cleaned up Robin's wound, he explained what had happened at the old quarry's edge, and how he'd left Peter there to think things through. Will had already said he'd seen men act like him before, men who'd been broken by war.

Marion was still angry. 'Any one of us could have gone after him instead.'

Knowing Marion was right to be cross, but also knowing that every instinct within him told him he needed to be the one who went after Peter, Robin changed the subject. 'Are they getting ready to take the abbot back?'

'Yes. Hugo won't like that Peter isn't to be arrested.'

'I don't care what he likes.'

Marion fastened a wrap of cloth around Robin's arm. 'How's that? Bandage tight enough?'

'Perfect. Thank you.' He kissed Marion lightly on the cheek. 'Could you stay here with Tuck, in case Peter arrives while we're taking Hugo back?'

'Of course. Be careful... that arm isn't up to firing a bow yet.'

CHAPTER FOURTEEN

Gerald de Grange, the Sheriff of Derbyshire, looked more or less as John Little remembered. His hair might have been grey rather than brown, and his skin lined with wrinkles that enhanced his appearance of general displeasure, but he was still staunchly proud and uncaringly dismissive of the world beyond the comforts of his manor—and the benefits provided by virtue of his noble birth.

'My Lord Sheriff,' John gave a small bow as he walked towards the cart upon which he sat. 'Forgive us for interrupting your journey.'

'Interrupting!' The sheriff's ruddy face glowed with anger. 'You ambushed us! Kidnapped my men!'

John looked over to where Nasir and Much were tying up the sheriff's guards. 'We'll let them go soon, don't worry. No one'll get hurt if you come along with us.'

'Come along with you? I'm not going anywhere with the likes of you, John Little!'

Father Harold stepped out from between the trees. 'I would if I were you, my Lord Sheriff.'

'Father!' De Grange's face contorted with rage. 'You said you'd come to warn me—not to betray me to such lowlifes! I'll have the Pope excommunicate you for this!'

'That is your right, my Lord.' Father Harold bowed solemnly, 'But please, first, come with us. It's time you saw that what you've been told about your sons is true.'

'That is not why I've come out here! I've told you before, I do not believe in idle gossip. No! I've only left the manor to see if I could…' He stabbed a thin finger towards Little John, '…catch him.'

'With respect, my Lord,' the priest smiled, 'that's not gone to plan. While you have ventured from the walls of your home, why not let us help you.'

'You are telling me that an outlaw wants to help a sheriff?'

As Nasir and Much came to his side, John said, 'It's come as much as a surprise to us as to you, De Grange, but your offspring are out of control… a messenger came all the way to Sherwood to ask us to come and teach them a lesson.'

'That's not your job!'

'No, it isn't.' Father Harold fixed the sheriff with a firm stare. 'That task should fall to you, my Lord, and yet, despite regular reports as to the Lords Aidan and Henry's conduct, you've done nothing about it.'

'How dare…?'

'My Lord Sheriff, you have two choices.' John's temper was becoming increasingly frayed as he gestured to the guards tethered to the trees. 'You can join your men while we go and fetch your boys and bring them here to talk to you, or you can join us for a trip to the tavern.'

'That's not a choice! I'm hardly going to agree to being tied up here with night approaching.'

'That's good, then.' Much grinned as he passed the sheriff a bundle of clothes. 'You can put these on now.'

'And what in Hell's name are these rags?'

'Clothes, my Lord.' Father Harold stepped forwards. 'You can't go to the tavern in your finery, you'd be recognised at once.'

'But…'

'Don't worry my Lord, you won't have to manage getting undressed and dressed all by yourself,' John smiled, 'Father Harold will help you change.'

'This is ridiculous.' The sheriff grumbled as he trudged his way along the path through the town of Hathersage. 'Why bother making me change when my face could be recognised anyway?'

'This is true, but you must admit, your usual clothing is distinctive. Far better to give no clue as to your presence.' John watched their surroundings carefully as they approached the tavern's door, keeping an eye on the folk going in and out. 'You will pull that hood up, my Lord. That way, your face will not be seen.'

As the sheriff did as he was told, Father Harold beamed. 'Stick close to young Much, keep your mouth shut, and we'll look after you.'

'What?' De Grange looked Much up and down with an expression that said he doubted this young boy could keep himself safe, let alone anyone else. 'But he's a child!'

'No I'm not!' Much protested. 'Am I, John.'

'Of course you're not.' John nodded to Nasir, who stepped away from the small group to keep watch in the shadows.

'Where is he going?' De Grange asked; fear beginning to gnaw away his usual confidence.

'Nothing to be worried about, my Lord.' John muttered, 'Nasir is going to make sure that we're safe. I'm sure you'd agree that's a good idea.'

'Safe from whom?'

'Your sons, of course.'

Sitting with Much at the back of the tavern, his hood still covering his face. Lord Gerald de Grange sipped from his tankard.

John muttered as he joined them. 'It's good to see that, unlike your offspring, you're welcoming the ale in here.'

The sheriff took another gulp of his drink. 'I've had better, I've had worse. I can't help but wonder if this is the last drink I'll ever have.'

Much's eyebrows rose. 'Why's that, then? Aren't you thirsty very often?'

'I was thinking more that you are notorious outlaws and all of England knows how you treat sheriffs.'

John snorted. 'I think you're getting things mixed up. It's more that the whole of England knows how the Sheriff of Nottingham treats *us*—not to mention his own people.'

'That however,' the priest cut in, 'is not why we are here. I suggest you sit back, enjoy your ale, and listen to the people here. *Your* people... the people you collect taxes from, the people who work the land for *you*.'

'I...'

'If you'll excuse me, I can see Thomas the Potter at the bar. I just need a word with him.'

A second later, Father Harold was at the bar. 'Thomas, how are you, my boy?'

'I'm worn out to be honest, Father.'

'Lots of people wanting new pots?'

'If only! And, even if that were the case, I've got next to no stock.' He took a draught from his tankard. 'You heard what those twin horrors did to my place last week?'

The priest shook his head, as if he had no idea. 'I've not. Tell me.'

'Lord Aidan and Lord Henry came into my workshop. No reason other than they were bored.' Thomas cradled his ale to his chest. 'Can you imagine having time to be bored?!'

'I cannot, but I suppose it is true what the good Lord has to say about idle hands making trouble.'

'And they are trouble to the bone! Trouble for the likes of me, anyway.'

Keeping one eye on the hooded figure, Father Harold pressed Thomas for details. 'What happened exactly?'

The potter had no sooner described how his workshop had been wrecked by the sheriff's youngest sons, when the taverner joined in with the complaints.

'I'd ban them, Father, but how can I? They're the lord's sons and they make the most of that and no mistake.'

'I heard they were in here the other night demanding claret.' Thomas sighed.

'Aye, that they were. As if anyone else in Hathersage has the pocket for such luxuries. By the time we've all finished paying for the damage they cause, there's not often enough for folk to buy food for their table, let alone an ale or two in here.'

Harold tutted loudly. 'As you both know, I've had reason to take them to task many times about pushing and shoving the locals as they walk or ride through the town, but it falls on deaf ears. It's bullying, pure and simple, but…'

The priest broke off as a shout broke through the air in time to the opening of the inn's door.

'You'd better have something suitable to drink

tonight, landlord, or be ready to face the consequences!'

Much and John felt the disguised sheriff stiffen as his sons barrelled into the tavern.

'That will be Lord Henry. I suggest you watch and listen, my Lord.' John whispered as the sheriff's youngest son shouted his threat to the landlord.

'My Lords, I have tried to explain, we just don't have the customers for claret.' The landlord held his position behind the bar.

'And *we've* tried to explain, many times now, that not doing as we ask has serious consequences.'

As Henry threatened the taverner, Father Harold spotted Nasir slink quietly into the inn, positioning himself by the door. Gaining strength from the outlaw's calm presence, the priest sent a private prayer to Heaven and moved closer to the bar. 'Now then, my Lords, please consider what you are doing.'

'Back off, priest!' Henry snarled. 'We've had to speak to you before about issuing unwanted sermons to your betters.'

Harold stood his ground. 'Your Lordships, what would your father say if he could see and hear you?'

The snort of laughter that shot from Henry's mouth echoed around the suddenly subdued inn. 'Very little, I imagine.'

'Your sheriff is a man of few words, priest.' Aidan sneered. 'Now, if you'll excuse us, we have a lesson to teach our host.'

Henry picked up the nearest tankard and threw it, hard, against the bar. The resulting crack sent pottery fragments flying in all directions and a spray of ale shooting to either side. As the locals jumped back, Aidan burst out laughing, before grabbing a jug and pitching it against the nearest wall—the contents exploding, making the nearby drinkers duck away from the flying shards.

'My Lords! Please!' The innkeeper watched in horror. 'I can't afford to buy new tankards, and I certainly can't afford to buy claret!'

'And we say, you can't afford not to!' Henry swiped a collection of half-drunk cups off the nearest table, sending them hurtling to the floor.

From their table, John growled, 'They're going to start a riot at this rate.'

The sheriff said nothing, but his hands bunched themselves into fists as he observed his sons in action.

'You stay there.' John hissed, as he got to his feet. 'Much.'

Without another word the two outlaws moved forwards, ready to intercept the customers deprived of their ale before they could attack the noblemen. The youngest of them was already shouting in protest.

'How dare you!?'

'We dare because we are the power here! You…' Henry sneered at the man who dared to stand before them, '…what do they call you?'

'Jack.'

'Well then, Jack, you are nothing.'

The slap of Henry's palm against Jack's face was immediately followed by a heavier retaliatory punch, from Jack—whose fist smacked Henry in the nose, sending a scarlet stream of blood across his tunic and cloak.

'No!' With a cry of protest, Father Harold dived between the brothers and the villagers—but not before Aidan had pulled his arm back, ready to deliver a blow to Jack's jaw.

Instead, the punch hit the priest full in the face, sending him sprawling across a nearby table, scattering the locals as he went.

'Uncle!' Little John, quarterstaff to hand, sprang into the fray as he called to Much, 'Make sure he's alright, I'll deal with them.'

Leaving a shocked sheriff behind them, Much went to Father Harold's aid as John raised his staff, aiming it at Aidan's stomach. 'Do not move!'

Meanwhile, Nasir placed a hand around Henry's neck, drew a knife from his belt and, with his usual calm poise, made the presence of his blade apparent as he pressed it against his prisoner's back.

'We told you to go back to Sherwood.' Aidan spat.

'And we told you to stop bullying the people of Hathersage. It seems that you didn't listen.'

'Neither did you.'

'True.' John called over his shoulder. 'How's my uncle, Much?'

'Broken nose. He'll live.'

Nasir tightened his grip on Henry's neck. 'You assaulted a priest.'

'Huh!' Aidan spoke for his brother. 'We taught a lesson to a meddlesome fool who should know better than to interfere in our business.'

The presence of the outlaws—weapons drawn—had sent a hush across the tavern. The innkeeper stood as if he was made of stone behind his bar. Thomas sidestepped away from the noblemen, nearer to the fallen priest, while Jack pressed a cloth against his face, blood soaking into its folds. No one else moved.

Thinking how much Henry reminded him of Gisburne, John asked, 'How disappointed would your father be if he knew of this?'

Aidan scoffed, 'How original! As if we haven't heard that before!'

'He wouldn't care.' Henry muttered from beneath Nasir's strangle hold. 'He doesn't even notice we exist.'

John saw a slight shudder come from the cloaked man at the back of the room. 'I doubt that's true. You are his sons.'

'Younger sons. Useless. Second rate. Unneeded. Unnecessary compared to our elder brothers.'

Unmoved by their self-pity, John placed the end of his staff flat against Aidan's chest. 'And this is you showing him you are needed, is it? By playing at being the town's thugs?'

'We're doing nothing of the sort!' Lord Aidan protested.

'The locals need keeping in their place. Father likes to stay in the manor with his home comforts, so—as the sheriff's sons—we've taken on that task. Making ourselves useful.' Henry muttered, his face contorted in anger. 'Our father would be proud!'

'He most certainly would not!'

Every person in the tavern turned towards the cloaked man, as his words ricochetted around the room.

'Father!'

CHAPTER FIFTEEN

Robin and Will kept their swords to hand as they led Abbot Hugo and his men towards the road to Nottingham.

'My brother is not going to like this.'

'So what?' Will gave the abbot's horse a slap on the rump, sending it skittering across the path, and Hugo grabbing at the horse's mane.

Robin smiled. 'You'll get the Fairfax land eventually, Abbot, and the sheriff will be glad not to have the expense of a trial.'

'You're probably right.' Hugo gave a shiver as they wove through some particularly densely packed trees. 'Where are we?'

'Near Darkmere... the old quarry...' Will waved a palm out to one side. 'It's not been used in years.'

'I left Peter up there, at the top, to think things over. Hopefully...' Robin stopped, a sense of foreboding hitting him only a second before he saw a figure bent out of shape on the ground ahead of them. Running forward, Robin hunkered down, sadness engulfing him as he realized it was Peter. 'I honestly thought he'd take the chance to live. To start again.'

A horrified Hugo dismounted and shuffled to the outlaw's side. 'You killed him!'

'I did no such thing.' Robin gave a sorrowful shrug.

'He didn't just fall down here on purpose. You took after him and killed him!' Abbot Hugo cried, accusingly.

Robin shook his head and was very quiet in his reply; 'He couldn't live with what he'd done.'

Scarlet wasn't convinced. 'Or he couldn't live with having to be poor like the rest of us!'

'I don't think so, Will. Somewhere Peter took a wrong turn—it could happen to anyone. Suddenly, I guess he saw what he'd become.'

Scarlet's head filled with a million images he'd rather never revisit. 'Taking an innocent life can take your mind. He lost it in France, I reckon. And then lost it again back here.'

'Are you saying he leapt to his death?' Hugo crossed himself before averting his eyes from Peter Fairfax's broken body.

'Taking lives can sometimes end with taking your own. He took his own.'

Robin laid a hand on Will's shoulder as he addressed the abbot. 'We take lives to survive. And to protect others. And then *only* when we have to. We *have* to stay strong for those that are not. Come on...'

Helping Abbot Hugo back into his saddle, Robin led them slowly away.

It was a rather subdued party that reached the pathway they'd been heading for.

'This is as far as we go, Abbot. The road to Nottingham is through those trees.'

'Good.'

'Oh, and Abbot.' Robin placed a hand on Hugo's right stirrup. 'If you and the sheriff have any ideas about taking Lady Fairfax's land for yourselves *before* they legally pass to you, then think again.'

'I would never...'

Will grabbed the stirrup on the saddle's left side. 'And we haven't forgotten about the use of your garden, Abbot. Tuck will be there tomorrow. If anything happens to him while he's helping himself, then your life will not be worth living. Understood?'

Hugo gulped. 'Understood.'

'Thank you.' Grinning, Robin took a step back from his horse. 'Then we will bid you a good afternoon.'

Without hesitation, Abbot Hugo yelled at the group trailing behind him. 'Men! Come on. For God's sake, let's get out of here…'

From the moment he'd left the outlaws behind him, Abbot Hugo's relief at still being alive had been tainted with thoughts of how to explain to his brother what had happened since he'd last seen him.

Even as he handed his horse over to the stable lad and strode through the castle, towards the great hall, Hugo was still wrestling with what to say—or, how to say it without incurring his sibling's maximum wrath.

Crossing the vast, servant-bustling space, he could see that the sheriff, Robert De Rainault, was sat—as he often was—at the high table; a goblet of claret in his hand, and a sour expression on his face.

Hugo took a deep breath. 'My dear brother. My dear... Robert. I have returned. With... er... news.'

'Ahhh, well don't stand on ceremony, Hugo, come closer. Let me pour you some wine.'

'Thank you, brother.'

As his footsteps clattered against the stone floor, the sheriff picked up a goblet. 'Now, let me give you your wine.'

Before he'd finished speaking, the sheriff launched the full vessel, throwing it at Hugo.

Shocked, the abbot stepped back in alarm, spluttering as he wiped the spray of wine from his face. 'Why, in God's name, did you do that? You haven't thrown wine at me since you were ten years old!'

'Because you're going to give me bad news, and I've been sat here waiting to hear it since Gisburne came back!' He grunted into his own goblet. 'He told me you forbade him from dispatching Fairfax! Where have you *been*, Hugo?'

'To the brink of death. I was lucky to survive.'

'And yet you did. Oiled your way out of the outlaw's grasp, did you?'

'Of course not!' Hugo shifted uneasily. 'How did you know I'd been captured by outlaws?'

'Your men-at-arms are rather faster to dismount and leave the stables than you are, Hugo! Servants in this place spread gossip quicker than a forest fire.'

Not bothering to argue, Hugo shook his gown free of wine splatter. 'Anyway, I am of the opinion that we're better off without the Fairfax Estates.' He spun round, taking his anger out on the staff. 'You, servant—I need wine to drink, rather than wash in!'

Hugo thrust out an arm, expecting a goblet of wine to magically appear, as his brother scowled in his direction.

'And since when have I courted your opinion on anything, dear brother? You answer to your faith, but I answer to the king. You know that he creates a special place in Hell for those that don't provide him with constant riches and gifts. I needed those lands!'

Greedily glugging down his wine, the abbot was resolute. 'I will not have anything to do with this.'

'Then Gisburne has earned himself a larger plot of land.'

'Then I wish you well trying to retrieve it, brother. Lady Fairfax is alive and well, and in possession of some form of black magic.'

The sheriff hesitated. 'Black magic?'

Hiding the spark of pleasure he got from wrong-footing his brother, Hugo nodded solemnly. 'She appeared as if a spirit before me.'

'I don't seem to be the only one with a full stomach of wine today.' Waving his goblet out in front of him, the sheriff shook his head in disbelief. 'Begone, Hugo. Get out of my sight! And if you see Gisburne on your way out, tell him to kick you up the backside as you leave.'

'Landlord! Close the tavern.'

The innkeeper broke his silence, 'Close it, my Lord? But…'

De Grange held up a hand. 'Fear not—it is only for tonight. You will be recompensed for your losses. In fact, the Lords Henry and Aidan will be paying for both your lack of income this evening, and for the breakages they've caused, out of their own purses.'

'Father!' Henry's mouth dropped open, 'How can you suggest that…?'

'That you take responsibility for your own crimes?'

'Crimes?' Aidan exchanged a worried glance with his brother. 'Hardly that.'

'Tell me,' The sheriff crossed his arms over his chest, 'how would you describe the assault of a priest, the breaking of goods, and the deliberate spilling of stock?'

'But, Father, we were helping you.'

Sorrow overtook De Grange's initial fury. He looked up at Little John. 'Thank you for bringing me here this evening. I didn't want to believe what I was told about these two... How I wish things hadn't been like this. Now I know the rumours were true, I shall take steps.'

'Steps?' Aidan's voice shook. 'What do you mean, Father?'

'I think it's time we found a use for you.'

Henry massaged his throat, sore from the memory of Nasir's grip. 'Use?'

Folding his arms over his chest, the sheriff stared at his sons in disgust. 'You can choose. Enlist in the king's army and go abroad, so you can at least use your lack of care for your fellow man in a useful way, or you can stay here and work on the land with the people until I consider your debt to them repaid.'

'What?!' The brothers spoke in unison—both horrified at either notion.

'You have until noon tomorrow to decide. In the meantime...' He raised a hand in Little John's direction, '... these good people will escort you back to the manor. And then they are going back to Sherwood. *Tonight*. Yes?'

'Yes, my Lord.' John glanced at his uncle, who was busy stemming his bleeding nose.

'Thank you, John.' The priest's voice, nasal and slow after his assault, rang with pride. 'You were great. Robin Hood will be as proud of you as I am.'

As the night sky dotted with stars, Much mused aloud. 'I wonder what they'll choose to do? Go to fight or stay and help.'

'They'll go.'

'I bet you're right, Nasir. They're far too proud to stay.' John pressed on, tired, but glad to be heading towards Nottinghamshire and Sherwood. 'Although, they're bullies—and bullies are cowards. How long they'd last as soldiers, I wouldn't like to say.'

Much was quiet for a moment. 'If they go to France, they might see the sorts of things Will saw—it might change them.'

'It will, lad.' John sighed, 'If they're lucky enough to return, we can only hope that it'll change them for the better.'

Much wrapped his cloak tighter around his chest. 'We didn't need the others in the end, did we? We managed on our own.'

Nasir gave the boy a small smile as he saw John nod.

'We did at that, lad. I'm sure they were needed there, just as we were needed here.'

'You ain't cross with Robin anymore, then, for not coming with us?'

'No, Much. And I shouldn't have been in the first place.'

'I wonder what the others have been up to while we've been gone?'

'I've no idea.' John scrubbed a hand over his beard, 'but I've got a feeling they'll be able to tell us who's the voice I heard was.'

'You think so?'

'Let's just say it's a hunch, Much.'

'It were right, though, Weren't it, John? It did happen tomorrow—well, today now.'

'It were indeed.'

Much grinned. 'And if Robin don't know who spoke to you, then I bet Herne will.'

'Very probably Much, very probably.'

EPILOGUE

Sat with his friends around the campfire, Robin held his hands up to the flames, feeling the comfort of their warmth. 'I owe you all an apology. I should have talked to you before I chased after Peter. I don't mean to make decisions without consulting you, but often—well, time is against us.'

Tuck hugged his arms around himself. He was feeling rather more shaken by recent events than he wanted to admit. 'Did Peter really kill himself, Robin?'

'I guess he couldn't come to terms with what he'd done. I did try to reason and help, but I wasn't expecting him not to return…'

Marion placed a comforting hand on Robin's leg. 'I think the Huntress knew what he'd do… or suspected, at least.'

'Maybe.'

Tuck crossed himself. 'May God rest his soul.'

The moment of contemplative silence that followed was only interrupted by the crackle of the fire, until Tuck voiced a thought that had been playing on his mind. 'You know, sometimes it's nice not to have to make the decisions.'

'Yeah… maybe.' Will continued to watch the dance of the flames. 'If you're gonna have a leader, then *they* can make the difficult ones.'

Robin threw a fallen twig onto the fire. 'I shouldn't have left him alone. I made the wrong decision this time.'

Still wrestling with the fact that Peter was dead, Will said nothing. He found himself unable to stop from thinking back to his own life in France and wondering how many more men had been cruelly conned in the same way Peter had.

'I wouldn't want any of you to have to make some of the decisions I have to make.' Robin climbed to his feet. His tone was heavy with regret. 'Sometimes I get things wrong—if I hadn't left Peter alone to think, then maybe….' His words faded into silence, before he rallied '… but that's no good. I don't have the luxury of thinking like that—*we* don't. But I know I'm very lucky.'

Scarlet looked at Robin as if he was mad. 'Lucky?'

'Yes.' Robin slipped his hands into Marion's. 'I'm lucky because I have all of *you* on my side. I know that you'll support me, no matter what. Whether I get it right or wrong. No battlefield commander has ever been so lucky.'

Tuck nodded wholeheartedly. 'Amen.'

Will snorted, but he couldn't help but smile at the same time. 'You should have met *my* battlefield commander.'

Marion grinned. 'Gave you a hard time, did he?'

'Yeah… Right tyrant 'e was… honestly, Robin… he'd clip you round the ear soon as look at you—and that's when he liked you!'

The outlaws laughed as, the mood lightning, Tuck lumbered to his feet to fetch them all some ale.

Will chuckled. 'You can laugh, but one time he grabbed me by the…'

Robin slipped through the forest towards Herne's Cave, now that Little John, Nasir, and Much had returned to camp. He'd listened to their story and been amazed that John had heard the voice of the Huntress.

No one had called him there, requesting his presence, yet he knew he was expected.

Striding into the cavernous space, he leapt over several puddles of water and followed the scent of fire-smoke to the heart of the Lord of the Tree's domain.

'Welcome, Herne's Son. You bring bad news.'

Robin stood before the Huntress. 'I wish I did not.'

'At least he is free from his turmoil now.'

'Perhaps.' He paused, before curiosity got the better of him and he asked, 'How did you survive the attack on the cart?'

At once, the blaze in the stone hearth quieted and the puddle-like pool began to stir, rippling despite the lack of draught.

'Herne found me. I was so near death—so badly injured by the sword wound, that only by taking on Herne's persona—by allowing myself to be immersed in his magic—could I begin to heal. Herne is a truly great spirit. He has sacrificed some of his power to save me.'

'I am honoured to be his servant.'

'You share his sense of self sacrifice. It's a rare gift.'

The stillness of the air abruptly changed, and a faint breeze ruffled Robin's hair and made the puddle ripple faster.

Unafraid, convinced the cave was responding to Herne, wherever he may be, Robin remained where he was. 'I suspect the sheriff will be after your lands, my Lady.'

'Lady Fairfax will return soon. She will be ready for de Rainault.'

'And Gisburne? He might find the cave again.'

A faraway smile of satisfaction appeared on the Huntress's face. 'No one sees the entrance the same way twice—unless they are Herne's Son.'

Robin looked down at the magical pool. 'I wish I'd been able to save Peter.'

'And yet, I suspect your instincts tell you, you could never have done that. The poison of what he'd done ran too deep.'

'Perhaps…'

The breeze that flowed through the cave quickened as Herne's voice suddenly reverberated around his home.

No, my son, there is no 'perhaps'. Take pride in your instincts; they serve you well.

Robin looked around him, searching for any physical sign of his master. 'Herne… where are you?'

Safe. I will be back when the Huntress returns to her rightful domain. I will always return… Always.

Also from Chinbeard and Oak Tree Books...

You may also enjoy...

Richard Carpenter's

ROBIN OF SHERWOOD

WOLVES OF
WINTER

P J Richards

www.ingramcontent.com/pod-product-compliance
Lightning Source LLC
Chambersburg PA
CBHW011511170626
46810CB00009B/3323